First published in Great Britain 2012
by Mills & Boon, an imprint of Harlequin (UK) Limited,
Eton House, 18-24 Paradise Road, Richmond, Surrey TW9 1SR

© Ruth Glick 2012

ISBN: 978 0 263 89526 1
ebook ISBN: 978 1 408 97232 8

946-0512

Harlequin (UK) policy is to use papers that are natural, renewable and recyclable products and made from wood grown in sustainable forests. The logging and manufacturing processes conform to the legal environmental regulations of the country of origin.

Printed and bound in Spain
by Blackprint CPI, Barcelona

"I feel as if I've ⬚ known."

Rachel laid her hand on ⬚ was thinking the same ⬚ ⬚ were wound up in a situation they didn't understand, chased by a murderer and the cops. But that was only part of it. They still had to deal with their ability to read each other's mind.

"Sealing the connection between us is our best shot."

"How do we…do it?" she asked.

"The usual way. With physical contact." Knowing he had reached the limit of his endurance, Jake hauled her into his arms.

She gasped as he pulled her against him but she didn't pull away. Instead, she clung to him with a desperation that echoed his own.

Again, it wasn't simply a guess about what she was feeling. He *knew*. He knew the exact touches that would bring her pleasure.

Unbearable heat threatened to overwhelm him. He felt as if he would die if he didn't make love with her…

Just then he sensed her fear and he knew she sensed his in equal measure.

And would he die if he did?

SUDDEN INSIGHT

BY
USA TODAY Bestselling Author
REBECCA YORK

(Ruth Glick writing as Rebecca York)

MILLS & BOON

Chapter One

You are going to die.

The words of warning clogged Rachel Gregory's throat as she sat across from the well-dressed woman who had come to her for a tarot card reading. Evelyn Morgan appeared to be in her late sixties, with dyed brown hair and carefully applied makeup, obviously a woman of a certain age who wasn't going to let time compromise the image she wanted to project.

And her mind was still sharp, because she instantly picked up on something in Rachel's expression. Leaning forward, she asked, "What is it? What do you see?"

To give herself a moment before answering, Rachel fiddled with a tendril of dark hair that had come loose from the French braid at the back of her head.

"I think you may have a rough patch ahead," she hedged as she looked down at the tarot cards again, hoping that her first impression was wrong.

Evelyn Morgan had selected them from the many different decks on Rachel's shelves, shuffled them, then made random selections before laying them out. She hadn't pulled the card most people associated with death, a black armored skeleton riding a white armored horse. But the Fool was there, upside down, which indicated the desire to strike out on a new adventure, although the journey could be disastrous.

The Nine of Wands was also reversed, showing that the man in the picture could barely take care of himself. And then there was the Hanged Man, contemplating making a sacrifice for the greater good. The Eight of Cups was also on the table, the card's image signifying dissatisfaction with the woman's present way of life. All in all, not a good outlook.

But the cards were never the only indicators for Rachel. She'd been doing this for fifteen years, since her early teens, and she always picked up more from the subject than the pictures spread out on the table.

Trying to pull her thoughts away from the woman's uncertain future, she said, "You're a visitor to the city. I think… you used to have a different name. Not Evelyn Morgan. You changed it after you left your previous job."

The woman's eyes widened. "You got all that from the cards?"

Rachel kept her voice even. "Well, the cards help me to… focus. To understand a person better."

"I'd call that more than understanding. You're coming up with facts that I haven't told you."

"Are they right?"

Ms. Morgan shrugged, and Rachel didn't challenge her. She hadn't expected confirmation. That was another thing about the customer sitting across the table in the comfortable wingback chair. She had secrets that she might or might not be willing to reveal to a stranger. Even when she'd come for a tarot card reading.

In this case, perhaps that was best. Because, if pressed, Rachel couldn't explain how she dipped into people's minds. Nothing deep. Only a superficial connection that gave her a glimpse into another person's biography.

Too bad she didn't have the same kind of insights into her own life. Or that she couldn't use the special knowledge to make solid connections with people. Sometimes she thought that she was doomed to drift through the days and years, snatching information here and there but never going deeper.

She'd picked up a bit more from Evelyn Morgan. She had apparently held an important position in a D.C. think tank before abruptly leaving her job and going underground. She'd lived very quietly, because she was running away from something or someone. But what?

Rachel wanted to ask about it, but she kept the question locked behind her lips. She wasn't doing this to satisfy her own curiosity.

At the end of the session Evelyn paid Rachel's fee and gave her a generous tip.

"I'd like to meet with you again," she said.

"Of course."

"I mean, I was hoping you could come to my hotel room tomorrow night—to discuss something with me in private."

Rachel looked around the cozy room where she did her readings. Before Katrina, she'd rented space in a coffee shop at the edge of the French Quarter, where the owner had let her read tarot cards for a percentage of her earnings.

After the devastation of the hurricane, when many people had left town, she'd been able to purchase and renovate her own place on Toulouse Street, partly with money an aunt had left her and partly with her own savings.

In addition to the readings that she did in the back room, she had a retail area out front where she sold various tarot card decks, magic wands, tea sets and other whimsical items that would appeal to New Orleans visitors.

"I prefer to work here," Rachel answered.

"I'm hoping we can have a more private meeting."

"Everything that takes place here is just between you and me. Nothing you tell me will go any further," she said reassuringly. Unless, of course, this woman wanted to tell her about a crime.

Ms. Morgan leaned forward and looked toward the door between the reading room and the shop.

"But anyone could wander in off the street and overhear us. Please make an exception for me tomorrow night." She paused, apparently considering her next words carefully. "It could be significant for you."

"A business contact?"

"I'm not going to talk about it here. Just give me the benefit of the doubt."

Rachel nodded. This woman obviously had something important to say. She didn't want to say it in public, but she was holding her breath, waiting for Rachel's answer.

"All right," she agreed, wondering what she was getting into. Because she had the sudden conviction that Ms. Morgan was telling the truth about the information being important to Rachel. Or at least that was part of the truth. The rest of it she was struggling to keep to herself.

They made an appointment for eight at the Bourbon Street Arms.

Ms. Morgan stood and took a few steps, and Rachel noticed what she'd seen when the woman had first entered—that she walked with a slight limp.

A sudden image flashed into Rachel's mind of a much younger Evelyn Morgan leaping off a bridge just before it exploded. And shattering her leg as she landed.

DRESSED IN A BLACK POLO shirt and faded jeans, Jake Harper was sipping a mug of strong, chicory-laced New Orleans coffee as he looked over the receipts from Le Beau, a restaurant he owned in the French Quarter. It wasn't his biggest business interest in the city, not by a long shot, but he liked working in the office at the back of the restaurant because the chef served him his favorites, like crawfish étouffée and oysters bienville for lunch.

Acquired tastes for a kid who'd run away from a dysfunctional foster home at the age of fifteen. In the seventeen years since, he'd carved out a niche for himself in the city's business community. Starting at the bottom, scrounging junk from back alleys and selling it to antique shops and dealers with tables outside the French Market. With his initial earnings, he'd graduated to garage-sale purchases and then estate sales. He'd bought his first antique/junk shop five years later—the same year he'd gotten his GED.

He might lead a comfortable life now, but the early experiences on the streets had made him tough and cautious. And always prepared for violence. In his experience, a situation could spin out of control with very little provocation.

He looked up as Salvio, the headwaiter, knocked on the door.

"Yes?"

"A lady wants to speak to you."

"About what?"

"Says it's personal."

"Young or old?"

The guy grinned. "Past her prime but keeping up appearances."

Well, it probably wasn't some chick trying to claim he was the father of her child. Not that he was ever careless about sex. He knew it could get someone into trouble faster than anything else.

Jake leaned back in his seat, wondering what the woman wanted. Maybe a donation for one of the charities he gave to on a regular basis? He'd slept in some of the city's shelters after he'd left his foster family, and he knew what it was like to live from hand to mouth, which was why he regularly gave back to the community.

The woman who walked in had a slight limp. She appeared to be in her mid- to late-sixties with dyed brown hair and a fully made-up face. She was nicely dressed in a summer-weight black suit and low heels.

She gave him a long look, as though she had been studying him and was interested to find out what he was like in person.

"Thank you for seeing me. I'm Evelyn Morgan." Her accent told him she was from somewhere in the mid-Atlantic region. Obviously not from a local charity, unless she'd just moved to the city and thrown herself into community activities.

He stood and shook hands. "What can I do for you?"

She half turned and glanced over her shoulder. "I'd rather not talk about it here."

"Uh-huh." He waited for more information.

"There's someone I want you to meet."

"Who?"

"It has to do with your…past, but I don't want to say any more."

He tipped his head to the side, studying her. "That sounds mysterious."

"I don't mean to be. Could you come to my hotel room tomorrow night at eight?"

He might have declined, but something about the way she lowered her voice made him hesitate. That and the sense of urgency she gave off. He was good at picking up vibrations from people—favorable and unfavorable. That was one of the reasons he'd been so good at climbing the success ladder. He usually knew when to trust someone and when to run as fast as he could in the other direction.

This time, he wasn't quite sure.

"You're not going to give me a clue?" he asked, calling on the charm that was part of his persona. When in doubt, sweeten them up with a little honey.

"I'm sorry. I can't talk about it here. But it's something

you'll want to know." She said the last part with conviction, then gave him the name of her hotel and her room number, before exiting as quickly as she had come, making him wonder what was really going on.

He waited a beat, then walked through the restaurant to the front door, staying in the shadows under the wrought-iron balcony above. She was about ten yards away, walking at a leisurely pace, stopping to look in the window of an art gallery. She turned her head one way and then the other, as though she was examining the paintings in the window, but he had the feeling she was really looking in the window's reflection, making sure she wasn't being followed.

He wasn't certain how he surmised that, but he was pretty sure it was true.

What was she up to? Some kind of scam? After watching her continue down the street and turn the corner, he went back to his office and sat down at the computer. When he put in the name Evelyn Morgan, there were several hits, but none of them seemed to match up with the woman who had come to him with her mysterious request.

Probably she'd taken the name recently.

He paused, wondering why he'd come to that conclusion on very little evidence. But he thought it was true.

He could skip the meeting, but the whole situation intrigued him, and somehow he knew he was going to keep the appointment.

In Portland, Oregon, a tall, white-haired man who now called himself Bill Wellington clicked on an email that had just arrived in his in-box.

Once, his office had been within sight of the Capitol building in Washington, D.C. He'd headed up a clandestine agency called the Howell Institute that had taken on some interesting jobs for the federal government and other entities that wanted discreet, reliable services performed.

Now he was nominally retired, living across the country, enjoying long lunches at the club and golf lessons—activities he hadn't had time for when he'd been playing the power game. He'd worked hard for thirty years, and he was taking advantage of the perks he'd earned. Like the name he was currently using. He'd been Bill Wellington for only a few years. When he'd been at the Howell Institute, he'd been someone else, a persona that he preferred to keep buried.

His occupation had put him in danger. In fact, he still had a few loose ends to tie up. And the email he'd just received had to do with one of them.

It read:

The woman you're looking for is going under the name Evelyn Morgan. She is currently in New Orleans, registered at the Bourbon Street Arms.

Because he'd learned not to get excited until he had all the facts, he went on to read the rest of the text, taking in details of her movements since she'd arrived in the Crescent City and studying the attached video clip that had been taken from across the street as she stepped into a restaurant called Le Beau.

The picture certainly looked like his former executive assistant, with a few years on her, although she'd dyed her hair brown and had some facial surgery to change her nose and her lips. But even with physical therapy, she hadn't been able to completely eliminate her limp. She'd been a daredevil in her time, and she'd shattered her right leg leaping off a bridge just before it had gone down in an explosion.

She'd been careful to stay out of circulation for the past five years, but Wellington had his sources, and he'd been confident that he'd eventually catch up with her. One of the men he kept on retainer had finally located her. She'd had a top-secret security clearance, and he'd trusted her with all sorts of confidential information—unfortunately.

She'd left with files that a more cautious man would have destroyed years ago. But Wellington was too much of a pack rat, and he wasn't willing to just forget about projects that might come back to haunt him in the present D.C. atmosphere where politicians set up a circular firing squad at the drop of a scandalous whisper.

He sat back in his chair, trying to put himself in Morgan's place. She was up to something, but did it involve putting the screws to her own boss?

For what?

Money.

He had no intention of paying. And no intention of leaving her roaming around on the loose where she could make trouble for him or drag the good name of the Howell Institute through the mud. He could have used the operative who'd sent the report on Morgan for the next part of the assignment, but he'd always found it better to compartmentalize. He went back to his computer and opened another file—this one a list of men he'd used for supersensitive assignments in the past. All of them were efficient and reliable.

Carter Frederick was in the New Orleans area, which meant he could get on the job quickly.

Wellington had never met the man in person. In fact, he dealt with him only through an alias—the Badger. Frederick didn't know who he really was and never would.

After dialing the number beside the name, he waited until an answering machine picked up.

"If you know your party's extension, you may dial the number at any time."

He punched in 991 and waited for a set of clicks.

Frederick came on the line. "How may I help you?"

"This is the Badger calling. I have a problem in New Orleans. A rush job."

"That will cost you."

He didn't like the guy's assumption that he was in charge of the conversation, but he was willing to overlook that, if he got results. "Not important. I'm having issues with a former employee. I want you to find out what she's doing there and what she knows."

"About what?"

"It's your job to get that from her."

"Better tell me a little bit more, so I'll know if she's spinning some kind of wild story."

"If I knew why she was in town, I wouldn't need you to question her."

"Okay. You got her location?"

He gave the hotel's name and address.

RACHEL SAW A FEW MORE clients, one a woman who came to her every few months for advice. She was glad to focus on the familiar customer so that she didn't have to think about Evelyn Morgan.

But finally she was alone again and unable to shake the sense of dread that had dogged her ever since she'd read the woman's cards.

She'd been sure Ms. Morgan was going to die. Could she tell her that, and maybe help her prevent it, if she did another reading when they met again tomorrow night?

After closing the shop, she went up to her apartment and busied herself fixing tuna salad, which she spread on some fresh greens and ate on the second-floor terrace adjoining her apartment while she looked through a catalog of new-age books she was considering for the shop.

Finished with the light dinner, she washed the dishes, then sat up in bed and read a romance novel for a while. She liked them for the intensity, for the emotions of the characters in relationships she was never going to have. Tonight, though, she was unable to keep her mind from wandering to Evelyn Morgan.

She finally gave up and lay in the darkness, trying to calm her nerves with relaxation exercises, but she knew she was definitely going to say something to Ms. Morgan tomorrow.

The decision was like a giant weight lifted off her chest. It was the right thing to do, and she was able to relax.

With a little sigh, she closed her eyes, and for a few hours she slept peacefully. Then she woke. Or did she?

She was lying in her bed, only she had the strange feeling that she wasn't really conscious.

Before she could puzzle that out, a shadowy figure stepped into her bedroom. A man. She couldn't see him in the darkness, but she knew he was large and solid.

She lay rigid as he walked toward the bed. In a shaft of light from the street, she got a look at him. He was tall and a little rough around the edges with dark hair and dark eyes.

He stood staring down at her, then glanced over his shoulder at something she couldn't see.

"We have to get out of here."

She shrank back. "Why?"

"They're after us."

"Who?"

He made a sharp gesture with his hand. "I don't know, but we have to leave before it's too late."

There was no reason to believe him. Then from downstairs, she heard the sound of a door quietly opening, and the realization of danger almost choked off her breath.

"Come on!"

He reached out and grabbed her arm, and a blaze of sensation shot through her, as if she'd suddenly grabbed a live electric wire, and the current was sizzling along her nerve endings.

But it was more than a physical reaction. So much more. Part sexual. Part longing. Part intimacy. None of which she could explain.

She'd never met this man before. Was he even real?

Yes!

It was like when she was reading the cards and she got a sudden insight into the person sitting across from her. Only this was so much deeper.

Did he feel it, too?

Yes.

He hadn't spoken. But she had heard the word in her head.

Before she could stop to consider that, he was urging her to leave.

Come on, he said again, another mind-to-mind communication.

She'd never experienced anything like it, nor did she know what to make of it.

But she got out of bed, wearing a sheer white nightgown that did nothing to hide her body from him.

He gave her a long, hot glance, and she knew that under other circumstances, they would be heading back to the bed, not away from it.

Instead, he led her quickly to the French doors.

They stepped out and ran across the roof, just as a man burst through the doors behind them, and she knew that if they didn't get away, they were dead.

The man who had first come to her room jumped nimbly down to the street level and held out his arms.

Without hesitation, she gave him her total trust, jumping into his embrace, crashing against him. He staggered back but kept his balance. When his arms came up to enfold her, she burrowed into him, feeling safe and at the same time more terrified than she ever had in her life. Not just because someone was after them. It was him. Them. Whatever was between them was going to change her whole life, and she couldn't stop it.

He lowered his mouth to hers for a hard, frantic kiss. As the contact deepened, something strange happened. She felt as though she was looking right into his mind, and the experience was like nothing she had ever imagined.

She opened for him, tasting him, taking in the flavor of man and fine wine.

She was so wrapped up in the experience that she had forgotten all about the guy on the roof, until his shadow loomed over them.

She saw it, even with her eyes closed.

Breaking away, she gasped.

Even though they were supposed to be running from an intruder, they had gotten wound up in each other. Now they were trapped.

She woke with a start, the dream leaving her feeling disoriented and scared and exhilarated, all at the same time.

She lay in bed, breathing hard, going over the details of the encounter. The man who had first come to her room had been familiar. She should know him. But she couldn't dredge up his name.

He had come to warn her that they were in danger. Was it a premonition? Or had she made it all up because she was upset about Evelyn Morgan?

RACHEL WAS RESTLESS ALL the next day and feeling as though she wasn't doing her best work for her clients. Finally, in frustration, she closed the shop and changed into a comfortable dress and low-heeled shoes before stopping to put on a little lip gloss and blusher.

The building she owned was several blocks from the Bourbon Street Arms, and she had plenty of time to change her mind as she walked through the winter New Orleans evening, past bars and restaurants, T-shirt shops and strip joints—that rich mix of French Quarter sights and sounds she'd known all her life.

It was still early, and the Quarter was crowded with tourists and locals out to have a good time, many of them walking along carrying cups of beer or mixed drinks.

Everybody appeared to be having fun, but she was feeling as if she were going to her own funeral.

Maybe she should just forget about this meeting, turn around and go home.

Since that wasn't really an option, she made her way through the crowd, pulled forward by the aura of danger surrounding the woman who had asked for a meeting that evening.

And not just around Evelyn Morgan. Rachel knew deep down that her disquiet had something important to do with herself, as well. And the man who had invaded her dream. Not invaded. He'd been the *reason* for the dream.

That was a strange notion, but again she couldn't shake it. Lost in thought, she turned the corner and stopped short, suddenly assaulted by the flashing red-and-blue lights of several police cruisers.

They seemed to be flanking the door of the Bourbon Street Arms, but she couldn't be sure because a crowd had gathered to watch the action.

"What happened?" she gasped as she stared at the cop cars and the bystanders.

"Don't know," a woman answered.

"Some lady's dead."

The breath froze in Rachel's chest. It was Evelyn Morgan. She *knew* it.

She brought herself up short. She didn't know that. Not

for sure, but she couldn't drive away the sick feeling gathering in her throat.

Uncertain, she looked around the crowd of gawkers. She could stay here, or go home and turn on the television where she might get more information than by hanging around.

She was starting to back away, looking to her right and left, when her gaze came to rest on a tall, dark-haired man who was craning his neck forward.

His features were a little rough around the edges. As though he'd done more living in thirty years than most men did in a hundred.

He drew near her, and she studied his blade of a nose, his hooded eyes, the shock of dark hair that he obviously had trouble controlling.

It was him. The man in the dream. Standing right on the street only a few feet away.

Oh, Lord, he was here, too, and no way could that be a coincidence.

As she stared at him, she realized what she hadn't been able to figure out after the dream. He was Jake Harper.

She'd seen his picture in the paper at charity events and at the opening of a new housing development for residents who'd been displaced by Katrina.

He'd interested her, and she'd done some reading on him. She remembered he owned some restaurants and antique shops and also a construction company. But he never talked about his background. She gathered he didn't come from money, but he'd worked his way into New Orleans society, although getting mentioned in the papers didn't seem to be his goal. It just happened from time to time.

What was he doing here?

The same thing she was.

As though he knew she was watching, he turned toward her, working his way through the press of bodies.

Just before he reached her, someone jostled her, and she almost lost her footing.

As she fought not to get trampled, Jake surged across the four feet that still separated them, catching her arm to steady her. And as his fingers closed around her flesh, everything changed.

A sizzle of electricity shot along her nerve endings, the way it had in the dream. She tried to jump back, but the crowd around her was too thick, and his grip was too tight for her to escape.

Chapter Two

Jake's heart was thudding, and at the same time his head was pounding. He wanted to let go of the woman, and at the same time he wanted to keep holding on to her forever.

The contradiction whirled in his brain along with a confusion of impressions that were more vivid than the street scene around him.

A shop in the French Quarter. Tarot cards. Tuna salad on a bed of greens. A woman alone in the swirl of humanity. Not just here but for as long as she could remember.

The thoughts came from her brain.

She was like him. Alone.

Her head turned toward him, her eyes wide with shock, and he knew that she was getting the same kind of impressions from him that he was getting from her.

Impressions and memories. Some of them recent. Others older.

A cute little girl walking home from school by herself. At the movies trying to understand the emotions of a love story. The same girl, sitting in her beautifully decorated room weeping.

Things that would be impossible for him to know, yet he was sure he wasn't making them up.

And under the thoughts and memories was an aura of

danger gathering like a dark cloud around them. Was she going to attack him?

Not likely. They'd met by chance in the middle of a crowd. Or was it by chance? Had someone sent her to ambush him?

Another image leaped into her mind. A woman with dyed brown hair. In her sixties. Walking with a limp. Wearing the same clothes she'd had on when she'd come to see him.

She was the only one who knew he'd be here.

"Evelyn Morgan," she breathed.

"What do you know about her?" he asked, hearing the shock and uncertainty in his own voice.

He'd forgotten the people around them. Now he remembered they were standing in the middle of a crowd, speaking in low voices, but they might as well have been alone for all the other people mattered.

The woman raised her chin. "She asked me to meet her tonight."

"Are you lying?" he demanded.

"Why would I?" she challenged.

Could she lie? After all, he'd pulled the information from her mind.

He held on to that extraordinary thought as he kept his hand on her, drawing her back through the mass of people until they had emerged into a clear space in the middle of the street.

A man in a wrinkled shirt strode toward the hotel. It was Detective Moynihan, whom Jake knew from his work with kids at risk in the city. "Detective," he called out.

The cop stopped and looked at him.

"What happened?" Jake asked.

"You know I can't give out any information."

Jake's hand was still on the woman. He was close enough to reach out with his other hand and touch Moynihan.

He wasn't sure why he did it, but as his fingers closed on the detective's sleeve, information leaped into his mind.

Evelyn Morgan. Lying in a pool of blood, her limp body on the floor of her hotel room.

Jake stared at him, struggling not to let the shock he felt show on his face.

"Got work to do," Moynihan said and pulled away, making for the hotel, leaving Jake alone with the woman.

"Let me go," she demanded.

"Not likely."

When she tried to wriggle out of his grasp, he held on to her, afraid she might run if he gave her the chance. Or was that her thought?

He wasn't sure. He'd never been less sure of himself in his life. Well, not in years.

He steered her a little way down the street, under one of the balconies that ran along the second floor of the buildings, providing shade during the day and shadows at night. His head was pounding, making it hard to think.

When they were alone, he dragged in a breath and let it out. "What just happened?"

"Evelyn Morgan was murdered."

"You picked that up?"

"Yes."

He hadn't been asking about the murder. That was a given. He was asking about the two of them.

"Will you take your hand off me?" she asked.

"Why?"

"You're making me nervous."

He dropped his hand to his side, ready to reach out again if she decided to turn and dash away. At least she looked as confounded as he felt. That was something.

"Who are you?" he asked.

She looked as if she didn't want to answer, but she finally raised her chin and said, "Rachel Gregory."

"You have a shop in the French Quarter," he said slowly as he recalled the mental images. "You read tarot cards."

She tipped her head to the side, studying him. "You researched me?"

"No. I picked that up from…your mind."

"Impossible!"

"Is it? Are you saying you didn't learn anything from me? You're the…psychic."

She sighed. "You're Jake Harper."

"You got that from my thoughts?"

"Actually, no. From the newspapers. You're a local celebrity."

"Oh, come on."

"What would you call yourself?"

"A businessman." He swallowed hard. "Let's cut to the chase. What's Evelyn Morgan to you?"

"She had a tarot reading yesterday, then asked me to come to her hotel room tonight." When he raised an eyebrow, she asked, "You don't believe me?"

"Actually, I do. Did she say what she wanted?"

"No."

"What time was that? I mean, the reading."

"Three o'clock. Why?"

"She had a busy afternoon. After she left you, she came to my restaurant, Le Beau, looking for me. She also asked me to come to her hotel room tonight."

This time it was Rachel who asked, "Why?"

"She said it was something personal. Something she couldn't tell me at the office. She said she wanted me to meet someone." He kept his gaze fixed on her. "I'm assuming it was you."

They stared at each other.

"We need to talk," he said.

She considered that. "What if I don't want to?"

"You're afraid?"

"Aren't you?" she retorted.

He gave her a hard look. "I always hope for the best and prepare for the worst."

"Which is what in this case?"

He waited until a couple walking along the street passed them. "I don't know. Let's get off the street. Le Beau is only a block away. We can talk there."

His heart started to pound as he watched her considering the suggestion. What if she said no?

What if she walked away from him? That thought made his chest feel hollow, but he told himself he knew where to find her.

When she finally said, "Okay," he relaxed a little, yet his nerves were still humming as he turned in the direction of the restaurant.

They walked through the darkened streets, neither of them talking nor touching each other, yet each of them giving the other sideways glances as though that would lead to a sudden revelation.

The restaurant was crowded when they entered, but the maître d' nodded at Jake as he headed straight toward the back, reassured by Rachel's footsteps behind him.

They walked into the same office where he'd talked to the now-dead woman.

In addition to the desk and chair, the room contained a small, comfortable seating area with a modern leather sofa, antique tables and an Oriental rug that he'd gotten from an estate sale. To the right of the sofa were a bar and lawyer's bookcases filled with old, leather-bound volumes that he'd bought when the aging resident of a Garden District Victorian had moved to a nursing home.

Rachel looked around with interest. "You're doing well for yourself."

He shrugged. "Moderately. Make yourself comfortable."

She sat down gingerly on the edge of the sofa, looking as if she could spring up and bolt at any moment. He understood why. The atmosphere in the little room had turned supercharged, as though their very proximity was about to set off sparks.

"I think we could both use a drink," he said.

"You have some wine?"

"Of course. What would you like?"

"Merlot."

"You have good taste," he said, thinking that sounded inane.

Turning, he opened the bar, got out a high-end bottle and removed the cork before pouring them each a glass. When he held one out to her, she said, "Put it on the table."

"Why?"

"Because apparently we read each other's minds when we're touching."

She'd said what they'd both been thinking.

He kept his gaze fixed on her as he sat down on the sofa, keeping several feet of space between them, even though he wanted to test the theory again.

"You're sure of that?" he asked.

"Aren't you?"

"I know what happened, but I'm having a little trouble believing it."

"Me, too."

He wanted to ask what she thought had happened, but he kept the question locked behind his lips. Instead, he studied her, trying not to be too obvious. She looked to be in her late twenties, with long dark hair pulled back into a French twist that was a bit undone so that a few wisps of hair hung down fetchingly. Her face was oval, her eyes large and blue. Her lips were very appealing. Too appealing.

He hadn't brought her to this private room for seduction. Or had he unconsciously had that in the back of his mind? Not a good idea. If touching her hand opened his mind to her, what would kissing her do? What about more than kissing?

He ruthlessly cut off that line of speculation before he could act on the feelings coiling inside him.

Shifting in his seat, he said, "You read people's minds all the time."

"I read tarot cards."

"And you pick up more than what's in the cards."

"How do you know?"

He shrugged, then gave her the kind of analysis he might give a business associate.

"Well, you support yourself as a reader. So either you're great at slinging bull…or you give people accurate information. I haven't seen you putting ads in the *Times-Picayune*, yet your business is thriving."

"I'm not into slinging bull."

"I didn't think so."

"But I don't have to live strictly on my income," she added, apparently wanting to make full disclosure. "I inherited some money from my parents and my aunt."

"They're dead?"

"Yes," she said without elaborating.

When she didn't volunteer anything else, he leaned back and tried to relax, which wasn't easy with whatever was humming between them. He wanted to reach for her. He wanted more than just his hand on her arm, but he wasn't going to tell her that. Not yet.

Of course, maybe she sensed it from the wary look she gave him as she took a sip of wine and set down her glass.

"I think we can assume that Evelyn Morgan wanted us to meet each other," he said. "The question is why."

She shrugged one shoulder.

"What if she came to New Orleans specifically to hook us up?" he asked.

"Why would she?"

"You have no idea?"

"No."

"Even after doing a reading?"

"No."

"And you never saw her before she walked into your shop?"

She shook her head.

"Let's stop playing Twenty Questions. I think there's a way to get some more information," he said.

When he moved toward her, she tried to scoot back, but he was too quick.

He reached for her shoulder and pulled her into his arms, then brought his mouth down to hers for a kiss that he wanted to be gentle. But gentleness was impossible as he folded her close.

He had seduced many women. He was good at making love and all the preliminaries. The sweet words. The touches. The kisses.

This time, he thought the woman might pull away.

When she stayed where she was, he felt a surge of elation. This wasn't simply seduction. It was a lot more important than a roll in the hay had ever been to him.

He liked sex as much as any man, but it had never held the kind of magic that people wrote songs about. It was physical sensation, nothing more.

He might have stopped to examine that idea, but he was too caught up in the pleasure of the moment as he increased the pressure, moving his mouth against hers with an urgency that shocked him.

He wanted her with a startling intensity, but a physical joining was only part of it. Sensuality leaped between them, carrying him deeper into unknown territory.

He had pulled thoughts from her mind. Maybe he'd been afraid it wouldn't happen again. But it did. Only this time there was more depth and clarity.

She had told him her parents were dead. He saw her as a woman in her early twenties standing in a small crowd at a cemetery, watching a coffin being lowered into a grave, and knew that her mother had died of a longtime heart condition. And Rachel had felt guilty because maybe her mom shouldn't have had children at all.

Her decision, he whispered into her mind

He saw her as a young girl, picking up a deck of tarot cards for the first time and feeling excitement surge inside her as she inspected the pictures and grasped the implications of the deck. This was what she was meant to do!

And at the same time, he heard her gasp and knew that she was pulling the same level of information from him. Things he had never told anybody. Things he had pushed down so deep that he'd thought they were buried for good.

He saw himself as a fifteen-year-old scrounging through Dumpsters at night for food, whacking at rats with a length of two-by-four.

Saw himself bedding down in an abandoned house, with the same two-by-four beside him as a defensive weapon.

Saw himself taking a discarded lamp to an antiques dealer and haggling over the price—getting less than it was worth but enough to keep him alive for a few more days.

"That's so sad," she whispered against his mouth.

"It's not true now."

"It made you tough and cautious. And determined to stay on top."

He didn't want to talk about his sordid past or her analysis of the man he'd grown into. He wanted to focus on what was happening now. In this room. With this woman who called out to him as no other human being ever had.

His head was pounding again, but he ignored the pain.

Wordlessly, he urged her to open for him. After a moment's hesitation, she did, so that his tongue could slip into her mouth to play with the soft skin inside her lips and sweep along the serrated line of her teeth, tasting the wine she'd just sipped.

She made a small, needy sound of approval as he deepened the contact.

While he stroked one hand down her body, he slid his mouth to her cheek, then found the tender coil of her ear with his tongue.

When she snuggled closer, he wrapped his arms around her and leaned back on the sofa, changing their positions so that she was sprawled on top of him, loving the weight of her small body and the way she fit against him. He wrapped her closer, increasing the pressure of her breasts against his chest, then sliding his hand down her back to her bottom so that he could wedge the cleft at the juncture of her legs more tightly against his erection.

When he did, she moved her hips against him, and he couldn't hold back a groan.

Her breath had turned ragged. So had his.

With any other woman, he would have been lost in the physical sensations.

Tonight the building sensuality couldn't stop the other part of it—the shocking part where her mind and his opened to each other in a way that should be impossible.

When a startling piece of knowledge leaped toward him,

he stiffened, then sat up so abruptly that she had to steady herself with a hand against the sofa cushion.

In the heat of the encounter, he had forgotten all about Evelyn Morgan. The reason Rachel had come to the Bourbon Street Arms. The reason she was here now.

They were supposed to be figuring stuff out, but it had gone far beyond that. Very quickly.

He heard the accusation in his voice when he said, "You knew she was going to die!"

ONLY A FEW BLOCKS AWAY Carter Frederick sat in the back booth of a bar. Dressed in a T-shirt and jeans, with a baseball cap pulled down over his eyes, he fit in with the casually dressed evening crowd. The Jazz Authority wasn't the most private spot in the world, but he needed a drink.

When the waitress brought him a double shot of bourbon, he chased it with a NOLA ale. He liked the local brew well enough.

He might have asked for more bourbon, but he wasn't finished working for the night, and he had to keep a clear head. In his mind, he was planning what he was going to say to the Badger, spinning it the best he knew how.

Evelyn Morgan had been a tough old broad. She had narrowed her eyes and refused to tell him why she was in New Orleans. Then she'd come up with some surprising moves.

He'd thought he could handle any woman. Not this one. She'd attacked, and they'd fought. When he'd pushed her away, the back of her skull had come down hard against the edge of the radiator. Too hard. One look at the blood pooling around her head, and he'd known that she was done for, and that he had to get out of there before anyone figured out that he'd been in her room.

Even so, he'd taken precious minutes to go through her stuff and make it look like robbery was the motive. While he was ransacking her luggage, he'd found a daybook with the names of two locals. Rachel Gregory and Jake Harper.

At least he had that much. Not enough to satisfy the Badger, but he'd already put off his report as long as possible. Anticipating a nasty few minutes, he signaled for the waitress and paid for his drinks.

When he was outside on the street, he lit up a cigarette and took several deep drags before tossing it away. Finally knowing he couldn't delay any longer, he pulled out his cell phone and speed-dialed a number in Portland.

The Badger answered, and he started talking before Carter could get any of his carefully planned words out.

"Unfortunately for you, I'm listening to CNN. A woman visitor to New Orleans was killed this evening. I guess you made an effing mess of the assignment," he said as soon as he heard Carter's voice.

"Not my fault. Why didn't you tell me she had martial arts training?"

"News to me."

The man might or might not be lying. In Carter's experience, the Badger said whatever was most effective at the time. And he might change his tune if another story was more convenient.

"Nobody can connect you with the incident?"

"I'm clean. I didn't talk to anyone at the desk. I paid a delivery boy to ask for her room."

"Okay."

"Afterward, I went down the back stairs."

"So you got away, but we're at a dead end."

"Not exactly. I got the names of two contacts that she visited in the city."

They talked for a few more minutes with the Badger pressing him for results and Carter wishing he'd never accepted the freaking assignment.

Not that he had a choice. Once you got on the Badger's Christmas-card list, you stayed on it.

After hanging up, he clamped his fingers around the phone as he automatically studied the evening crowd to make sure nobody was listening in.

Then he started planning his next moves.

Chapter Three

Rachel dragged in a breath and let it out. "I saw something in the cards."

"Her death?" he clarified.

"I thought so. But it's never hard and fast. There are always alternate interpretations of anything I see."

He swore under his breath. "You were thinking, 'You're going to die.'"

"But I couldn't say it. Not like that."

"Did you warn her?"

"No."

His voice turned sharp. "Why not?"

Rachel couldn't help being defensive. "Would you tell anyone something that devastating? I could have been wrong. I never tell people anything so…upsetting. I let her know she was in for a rough patch. At the end of the session, she asked me to meet her at her hotel room tonight."

"Oh, yeah?"

"You think I'm lying?"

"No."

They had been so close a moment ago. Too close, and they must have been thinking the same thing. It was time to put up some barriers.

She moved away from him and automatically felt to see

if her hair was messed up. Some had come loose, and she worked stray strands back into place.

Her head was throbbing, making it hard to think.

"Coming here was a mistake," she said as she stood up and smoothed out her dress.

He kept his gaze on her. "Something happened between us. Don't you want to find out what it was?"

"Lust."

"You know damn well it was more than that."

Maybe she did, but she wasn't going to admit it to him. Not now. Not when she was still shaking inside from the intensity of what she'd felt—on so many levels.

Turning on her heel, she left the office and walked through the restaurant, feeling the eyes of the maître d' and some of the diners on her.

She kept walking, out onto the street, then headed back toward her building. The shop door was on Toulouse Street. The entrance to her apartment was in a little courtyard with an iron gate. She unlocked it, glad when the light came on as she stepped into familiar surroundings.

She'd fixed up the area with potted plants and patio furniture. Sometimes she sat down here; sometimes up on the upper patio outside her living room. Tonight she just wanted to get inside her apartment and lock the door.

When she was finally feeling safe, she sat down at the table by the window and stared out into the darkened street, trying to figure out what had really happened tonight.

A woman had been murdered. A woman she'd done a reading for a little over a day earlier.

Was Jake Harper's harsh judgment right? Should she have warned Evelyn Morgan about what she'd seen? Had she played a role in her death by keeping silent? Maybe Evelyn would have left New Orleans. Maybe that wouldn't have done any good, like in that book *Appointment in Samarra,* where the guy is heading for death no matter what he does.

She squeezed her hands into fists, grappling with the what-ifs.

She came back to the woman herself. There had been a strong streak of determination in Evelyn Morgan. She wouldn't have run. She would have stayed around to accomplish her mission—whatever it was—but maybe she would have moved up her timetable. What if the meeting had been last night and Evelyn had left town before her murderer arrived?

Rachel had never felt so conflicted about a reading. True, she'd seen death in the cards before. But not murder.

Well, she hadn't known it was murder. The cards hadn't been that specific. And as she'd told Jake, there was always the chance she'd gotten it wrong.

She squeezed her eyes shut, struggling to banish the woman's image from her mind. As she tried to focus on something else, her thoughts jumped back to Jake Harper. Another upsetting subject. For too many reasons.

All her life she'd felt a little apart from other people. No, to be brutally honest, she'd felt a lot apart. People made connections that she simply couldn't manage herself.

Over the years she'd had lovers. The physical part had been all right, but she'd longed to find a soul mate—someone who would understand her and be there for her no matter what happened.

It had never come to pass. Somehow, she always put emotional distance between herself and other people because it felt as though something was missing in the relationship. Did she create that? Or was she missing some cues about human relations that came easily to everyone else?

When she and Jake Harper had met on the street, when

they'd touched, she'd felt a zing of awareness that was totally alien to her.

She'd wanted to burrow into his arms. At the same time, she'd wanted to run from him. But she'd gone back to his restaurant, and when he'd started stroking her and kissing her, everything from the encounter on the street had only become more vivid.

She'd felt a need for him that burned in her brain and in her blood. Even though it had frightened her, she'd clung to him.

The need had been the same with him. She knew it from the way he'd kissed her with an urgency that took her breath away. And from what she'd read in his mind. He was a man, and lust should have been enough to keep him focused on what they were doing.

Instead, when he'd stumbled on the information that Rachel had anticipated Evelyn's death, he'd pulled away.

Because he was shocked that she hadn't warned the woman? Or because the intimacy had triggered that Vulcan mind-meld thing, and he'd been as confounded by it as she?

She wanted to ask him. At the same time she heard an inner warning to stay as far away from him as she could.

And then there was the headache. Had the intimate contact been responsible for that, too? And made it hard to think clearly?

Trying to wrest her mind away from Jake, she crossed the room and turned on the television set. The hotel death had made the evening news.

But there wasn't much more information than they'd picked up on the street. A woman had been found dead in her hotel room when the maid had come in to turn down the bed and put a piece of chocolate on the pillow.

Rachel fired up her laptop and got a web account of the incident. When she didn't find anything new, she picked a

deck of tarot cards from the shelf beside her easy chair. She
had collected them over the years. There were modern interpretations. Fantasy versions. A Gothic deck with witches and
vampires. But she usually ended up going back to the Rider-
Waite deck because that was what she'd learned on, and she
knew the cards so well.

She had never been good at doing readings for herself.
Particularly anything formal. Instead of laying out one of the
classic patterns, she shuffled the cards and cut, pulling out
one at random.

The Lovers. Oh, great. Apparently she couldn't get away
from the heated scene between herself and Jake Harper.

Were they getting together again?

She shuffled a second time, and got the Magician. Did that
mean she wanted to find a new direction in life? The card
said that everything she needed was there—if she wasn't
afraid to reach for what she wanted. She had the tools and
the power. Or did she?

IN BALTIMORE, MARYLAND, Mickey Delaney sat in front of the
television set, waiting for Tanya to come home from one of
her shopping trips. She liked to buy things. A lot of the time
it was things she didn't need, like clothing or jewelry, but he
didn't complain. What was the harm? If it made her happy,
let her spend money. They could always get more.

"Yeah, money's not a problem," he said aloud just before
an item on CNN caught his attention.

He'd turned it on because he liked to keep up with stuff.
Now one of the talking heads was giving an account of a
murder in New Orleans.

"The woman found dead in her New Orleans hotel room
yesterday has been identified as…"

"Evelyn Morgan," Mickey said.

The name had leaped into his head before the guy said it.

He didn't know why, but he waited to see if the announcer said the same thing.

"Evelyn Morgan."

"Okay!"

"She has no known relatives, and her reasons for being in the city have not been established, but it appears that robbery was the motive."

Mickey was still focused on the way he'd picked up her name. It was like knowing the phone was going to ring and knowing who would be on the other end of the line, but this seemed more important than a phone call.

A little jolt of fear sizzled through him.

Was Evelyn Morgan going to mess up what he and Tanya had? Was that why he'd known her name?

Mickey shook his head. Sometimes when he woke up, he had to pinch himself because he couldn't believe that his new life was real. As a kid he had to endure the constant fighting of his parents. He was using drugs by the time he was fourteen. When good old Mom and Dad had kicked him out, he'd hooked up with some of the dealers on the street in Baltimore.

Big business for the bosses. Small potatoes for the working stiffs.

He'd met Tanya Peterson at a Twelve-Step meeting after he'd gotten into some kind of do-good program run by a city charity.

They'd helped him clean up. Gotten him an apartment. But he'd known he was going to slip back into the bad life—until Tanya.

The first time they'd met, they'd clicked in a way he didn't understand. It had been like a hit of some exotic drug, and he'd wanted more. Their thoughts had started running along the same lines—just like that.

They'd robbed a tourist down by the Inner Harbor, then gotten a hotel room where they could be alone.

They'd taken the money and headed for Chicago. Followed by Atlanta. New York. Cleveland.

Now they were back in Baltimore in a furnished Federal Hill town house they were subletting by the month because Tanya had gotten a yen for Maryland seafood.

She was going more on whims lately. Which was starting to worry him, and he hoped to hell that she wasn't going to screw things up for the two of them.

When the door opened, he looked up. She had a couple of shopping bags with her, from Nordstrom and Macy's and a couple of those high-priced women's specialty shops.

She dropped the bags on the floor and crossed to him, just as the guy on TV started in about the murder again.

Tanya went very still. "I don't like that at all."

"It's nothing to do with us," he answered, hoping it was really true.

"I think you're wrong. It's got to do with us, and it could be...bad."

"How?"

"I don't know yet. But we're going to find out before everything changes."

The warning sent a shiver over his skin. He loved things the way they were. No way did he vote for any changes. Well, if he could have anything he wanted, he'd like it if Tanya could just relax and take things the way they came. But he didn't hold out much hope for that.

THE MURDER OF EVELYN MORGAN and the encounter with Jake Harper had put Rachel in a strange mood. Usually she looked to the future. Now, before she went down to open the shop, she started rummaging in the storage closet at the back of her apartment, where she kept some of the mementoes she'd brought from her parents' house after Dad had died.

She took out an old photo album and thumbed through it,

studying the pictures of herself and her parents when she'd been a baby. They looked so proud and happy to have her.

Seeing their faces gave her a little pang. Things hadn't turned out the way they'd expected. She hadn't exactly been the daughter they wanted. She'd never been warm and cuddly with them. She hadn't made friends with kids in school, and when she'd gotten interested in tarot card reading, she'd seen their disapproval. At least they hadn't forbidden her to work with the cards, but they'd insisted she graduate from college before she could become a full-time reader. Which was why she had a useless degree in history.

She turned more pages in the album, looking at pictures from the early life that she barely remembered. There was a picture of her at about age three with Mom outside a white building, with a plaque beside the door. She could see the word *clinic,* but she couldn't read the name of the place because a tree branch partly hid it.

She clenched her fists in frustration. Intuition told her the name was important, but it looked as if whoever had taken the picture had deliberately made the sign unreadable. Could someone scan the photo and enlarge it?

Maybe, but she wasn't going to take it to a photo shop or a computer store. That would be dangerous.

Dangerous?

She wasn't sure where that conviction came from, but in this case, she trusted her instincts and went back to the albums, looking for a picture taken at the same place. When she couldn't find any, she gave up.

Finally, she snapped the book closed and sat with it on the table in front of her, staring into space, thinking about Jake Harper—the subject she'd been trying to avoid since last night.

JAKE HAD PLENTY TO DO TO keep himself busy over the next twenty-four hours. Like several businesses to run. With the restaurant, his assistant, Patrick, who'd been trained in one of the country's top cooking schools, did the major work like ordering supplies and overseeing the kitchen.

But Jake was the one who knew antiques, and he did have to inspect an out-of-town shipment that a dealer had given him first dibs on.

He was usually good at bargaining. This time, though, he couldn't focus on Victorian desks and Queen Anne dining room sets because his thoughts kept zinging back to Rachel Gregory.

Finally he made an offer on the furniture, just to satisfy the dealer. When the guy's eyes widened, he knew he'd paid too much, but he wasn't going to go back on the deal.

He left as quickly as he could, hardly aware of his surroundings as he started thinking about the woman from last night again. They'd been heading for lovemaking before she'd left. And it was his own damn fault that she'd fled. Maybe if he hadn't been so harsh, if he'd just kept his damn mouth shut, they would have ended up finishing what he'd started.

Or would they?

He'd wanted her—more powerfully than he'd ever wanted any other woman. Yet at the same time, as the heat had built between them, he'd felt the edge of danger. If he made love with her, it was either going to be the best thing that had ever happened to him…or the worst.

And when he'd read the information about the dead woman in Rachel's mind, he'd used the excuse to pull away.

Unfortunately that hadn't stopped him from thinking about Rachel, almost to the exclusion of everything else.

Telling himself he wasn't obsessed, he searched her on Google and found out that she'd been reading tarot cards in the city for about fifteen years. She'd started as a teenager on summer school breaks and quickly developed a reputation that brought customers coming back and recommending her to their friends, just as he'd surmised.

She'd stayed through the aftermath of Katrina, and she'd been able to pick up property in the French Quarter at a reduced price—leaving her in a very good financial position. She made money from her readings and also from the tourist items she sold in her shop. And she also had her inheritance.

In addition, she'd made good investments.

Because her profession gave her advance market information?

Maybe.

He laughed. He could use someone like that on his staff, giving him hot tips. But he doubted she'd want to work for him.

He tried to get her out of his mind, but finally he gave up. They'd left a lot of stuff unanswered when she'd fled his office.

What if he went over to her place and asked her some questions? He laughed, then sobered. If he asked for a reading, was she going to make the price so high that he'd turn around and leave? Or was she going to tell him he was marked for death?

He tried to shove those thoughts out of his mind, but he couldn't do it.

Finally, just before five, he told Patrick he would be out for a while and walked into the street. It was almost dark, and he didn't need a pack of tarot cards to feel a sudden sense of dread.

He looked around, expecting some kind of trouble on the block, but saw nothing.

He'd planned to stroll to Rachel's, but a leisurely walk was suddenly out of the question. He had to get there fast. He had a choice of cars and trucks, but since he didn't need them in the French Quarter, they were all in garages several blocks away. By the time he got a vehicle and drove to her shop, it would be too late.

Too late for what?

He wasn't sure, but he knew he had to get to her. Now.

He started running, dodging around a couple who were holding hands, taking up the whole damn sidewalk.

"Watch out, buddy," the man called.

Jake didn't bother with a reply. He just kept running.

RACHEL HAD GONE DOWNSTAIRS and opened up in the afternoon. She saw her last client at four-fifteen, a woman named Mrs. Sweet, who'd been referred to her by a friend. The new customer was from Denver, and she was excited about coming to New Orleans to see "the great Rachel Gregory." The adulation from a stranger was embarrassing. She didn't think of herself as great—just a woman who picked up insights that others might not see.

Trying to live up to the advance reviews, she did her best to give a professional reading. To her relief, as far as she could tell, Mrs. Sweet didn't have any problems in her future. In fact, her son was going to tell her soon that she was expecting her first grandchild. Rachel was pretty sure it was going to be a boy, but she didn't go out on a limb and say so, in case she was wrong because she wasn't exactly concentrating as well as she should. Even when she was focusing on the cards the other woman had drawn, Rachel's mind kept wandering to Jake Harper.

Had it been a mistake to run away from him? She wasn't sure, but she had the sense now that she needed him.

For what?

When Mrs. Sweet left, she straightened up the room where she did her readings. Everything here was familiar to her. The comfortable high-backed Queen Anne chairs and square table where she and her customers sat. The muted colors of the stained-glass lamp hanging in the corner. The lacy curtains at the window.

She'd decorated the room for her own pleasure and to create what she thought was a charming atmosphere for clients. Usually, sitting at the table alone gave her a sense of peace. Today she felt restless, as though a thunderstorm was building. Not in the air but in this room.

Which made no sense.

She shuffled the cards again, turning them up at random the way she'd done the day before. She got the Lovers again. Then the Seven of Cups. The card showed a man trying to decide among the objects in several goblets. A castle, jewels, a victory wreath. And one cup with a drape over the top so there was no way to know what was inside.

It all represented emotional choices. Difficulty making decisions. Which was a good description of her present state—at least with regard to Jake Harper.

She was studying the card, trying to see more in it, when a noise in the front of the shop made her go still. She'd locked the door after Mrs. Sweet, but it sounded as if someone was out there, moving stealthily toward the room where she sat.

She might have called out. Instead, she got up and started for the back door. Before she reached it, a man stepped into the room where she was sitting.

He was holding a gun, pointed at her.

"Hold it right there. Hands in the air."

With no other choice, she raised her hands, studying him. He looked to be in his late thirties. His hair was blond, his eyes were icy blue. She would have noticed him if she'd passed him on the street. There was something in his face that made her shiver. Up close his dangerous aura seemed to pulse around him.

"What do you want?" she asked, struggling to keep her tone even because she sensed that he wanted her to show fear.

He liked a woman's fear. She didn't have to read his cards to understand that. Not this close to him.

"I'll ask the questions."

She swallowed. "I don't keep much money in the shop."

"I don't want money."

"Then what?" she asked, playing for time. Why? What was going to change in the next few minutes? She couldn't answer, but she knew it was important to keep him from hurting her. Because she sensed something just outside her reach. Something that would help her.

"You know Evelyn Morgan," he said.

"I don't know her."

"You're lying. Your name was in her daybook."

She raised one shoulder. "She came here. I did a reading for her. That's all."

"You're lying."

She struggled to keep her voice even. "Why would I lie?"

He made a rough sound. "You know she's dead, and you don't want to get involved."

And he was the man who had killed Ms. Morgan, Rachel knew with sudden conviction.

He kept speaking. "Or you have information that you want to keep to yourself. Either way, we'll get to the truth. Sit down."

When she moved to one of the Queen Anne chairs, he gestured toward the ladder-back against the wall.

"Over there."

She sat with her heart thumping inside her chest, watching him as he pulled a set of handcuffs from his pocket and tossed them to her. She caught them and clattered them in her hand.

"Put them on."

His total focus was on her, so that he didn't see the flicker of movement behind him.

Chapter Four

Rachel clanked the metal cuffs in her hand.

"Stop playing with those damn things and put them on!"

She kept moving the metal links in a hypnotic rhythm, willing him to watch her, holding his focus and struggling not to give anything away.

The man who had appeared behind the intruder was Jake Harper, standing like a coiled spring in the doorway, taking in the scene, a grim expression on his face.

She kept her gaze on the guy with the gun. "I don't know anything about Evelyn Morgan besides what I saw during the reading."

"We'll see. But first we're going to get comfortable." He laughed, a grating sound that raised the hairs on the back of her neck. "At least I will be. Put on the handcuffs if you don't want to get shot."

The man might be enjoying his power over her, but if he wanted information, he wasn't going to shoot her. She hoped.

Still, questions whirled in her mind. Why had he killed Evelyn Morgan? Because she hadn't talked? Because she'd told him something incriminating? Or had he gotten too rough and done it by accident?

Her heart was pounding as she lifted the cuffs in her fingers, still making the links click together.

"Stop stalling."

Instead of snapping one of the bracelets around her wrist, she threw them on the floor, watching from the corner of her eye as Jake silently picked up a heavy glass paperweight from the display shelves.

"You witch. You're going to be sorry," the man growled. "Get down on your knees and pick them up."

As she slipped off the chair, getting on all fours and drawing the man's gaze downward, Jake leaped forward, striking the intruder on the back of the head with the paperweight. She'd already dodged to the side as the weapon discharged, and the man went down in a heap in the middle of the floor.

Jake ducked around him, pulling her up. "Are you all right?"

The feeling of relief was overwhelming. Relief and more. As he held her in his arms, they exchanged silent messages.

You knew something was wrong.

Yeah.

Thank you for getting here in time.

You kept him busy.

She wanted to stay in Jake's arms, but she knew that the feeling of safety was only an illusion. They had to get out of here.

Her eyes flicked to the man on the floor, seeing the blood oozing from his hair.

"You hurt him."

"Not as much as he was planning to hurt you. Head wounds bleed a lot."

She winced.

Jake squatted beside the man, picked up the gun and handcuffs and cuffed the guy to a heating pipe.

Next he handed her the gun. "Keep him covered."

She accepted the weapon, wondering what would happen if she had to shoot it.

Jake felt for a pulse in the guy's neck.

"Is he alive?"

"Yes." He rifled through his pockets and pulled out a wallet. In it were a driver's license and a couple of credit cards in the name of Eric Smithson. He also took the hand-cuff key.

"Probably the ID's not in his real name," Jake muttered. "Give me the gun."

She was glad to hand it over and watched as he switched on the safety and tucked it into the waistband of his jeans.

"We can't leave him here," she whispered as she stared at the assailant. She was still coming to grips with what had happened and what would have happened if Jake hadn't arrived.

"You want to call the cops?" he asked, his voice hard.

She considered that option. "No."

"Why not?" he pressed.

She'd always been a law-abiding citizen. Now she heard herself answer, "I don't want to get myself connected to the Evelyn Morgan case."

"Agreed."

"What should we do?"

"Well, you can't hang around here. Too dangerous. Can you stay with a friend?"

She thought for a moment and couldn't come up with anyone she could impose upon. Not when she was hiding out from a guy who was probably a murderer. And she was pretty sure Jake could guess what she was going to answer.

When she shook her head, he said, "You're staying with me."

Undoubtedly what he wanted.

She swallowed. "Okay."

"Go up and pack a few things."

"You know I live upstairs?"

"Yes."

She didn't comment as she turned toward the door that led up to her apartment. Jake hesitated, then followed.

She stood for a moment in the middle of the darkened room, feeling paralyzed, her brain in danger of shutting down. Which wasn't an option.

Grimly she forced herself into action, taking underwear and some practical clothing out of drawers, then throwing a few personal items and some makeup into a small kit.

After she'd stuffed everything into an overnight bag, she looked up to find Jake watching her and holding the gun he'd taken off the assailant.

"What are we going to do with the guy down there?"

He thought for a moment. "Take him to another location and turn the tables on him."

"You mean question him?"

"Right. I'd like to know who he's working for."

"If he killed Evelyn Morgan, won't he be…dangerous?"

"I think I can handle him," Jake said, and she knew from the tone of his voice that he'd taken care of a lot of business she didn't want to ask about.

When she started for the stairs, Jake held her back. "Stay behind me."

He hurried down the steps, then stopped short as he reached the ground floor, muttering a curse.

WHERE THE HELL WAS CARTER Frederick? Bill Wellington expected a second report from the man, but perhaps it was too soon.

He hadn't been willing to reveal what he wanted to find out from Evelyn Morgan, but he already had a hunch it might be connected to a cockamamie medical research project the Howell Institute had funded years ago.

To give himself the illusion of progress, he started accessing medical reports from the Crescent City and the surrounding area. At first there wasn't anything of unusual interest. Then he began to pick up a strange set of data. On deaths from cerebrovascular accidents among young adults in New Orleans.

There were more than you'd expect in the metropolitan area. And when he checked to see the individuals involved, he found that many of the deaths came in pairs. All those victims were unmarried couples in their late twenties or early thirties. Young men and women who were found in bed together.

Did Evelyn think that Rachel Gregory and Jake Harper were going to be the next victims? Was that why she'd showed up in New Orleans?

That was certainly a stretch, but why would Evelyn have been trying to contact them? Was there some new kind of brain disease going around Louisiana, and she thought those two had contracted it?

Because a Howell Institute project had made them susceptible?

He reached for the phone and called Carter Frederick. No answer. Again. Did that mean the guy was in trouble? Or was he avoiding making a report because of another screwup?

Wellington slammed a fist into the palm of his opposite hand. He didn't like being jerked around, and he didn't like operating by remote control in Portland.

When he'd been running the Howell Institute, he'd had more trustworthy operatives. Retirement had forced him into using less reliable guys, and now he was paying the price. If he didn't get results this way, would he have to go to New Orleans himself and do it right? But was that worth the risk?

As RACHEL PEERED AROUND Jake, she saw what had made him curse. The man on the floor was gone, leaving a small pool of blood where his head had been.

"He was cuffed to a heating pipe," she said.

Jake swore again. "I guess he had a spare key."

"Will he go to the police?"

Jake barked out a laugh. "He came here to harm you. And he probably killed Evelyn Morgan. I hardly think he's going to call the cops."

"He could make up some story."

"You think?"

"Okay. No." She looked at the blood on the floor. "But he needs medical treatment."

"Like I told you, head wounds bleed a lot, so it may be superficial. But if he goes to a doctor, he'll make up a story about what happened."

She kept staring at the blood. "I have to clean up."

He made a rough sound. "I'll send a cleaning crew over. Just lock up after us and put up the closed sign."

He moved to the side of the door and looked out.

"You don't see him?"

"No. And now we're really getting out of here."

He stepped outside, waited a moment and motioned for her to follow.

"Where are we going?"

"A place I own."

"Your house?"

"No. If he could find you, he could find me."

"Does he even know who you are?"

"We have to assume he does, even if it's not true. Which means we're going to a different location."

"A hideout?"

He laughed. "It's a set of converted row houses where I store antiques that aren't going right to my shop. But the top floor was already outfitted as a loft. I go there sometimes when I need a change of scenery."

He led her rapidly away from the shop, and she hurried to

keep up. To her relief, he slowed his pace when they turned the corner. There were only a few people on this street, and she glanced at them as they passed. Nobody seemed to be paying attention to her and Jake Harper.

Still, he took a circuitous route through the French Quarter, ducking down alleys and stopping to listen and look behind them every so often. He had an excellent knowledge of the area, and as far as she could tell, no one was following them.

They ended up in an alley a few blocks away, where he stopped at a three-story building that was as wide as three town houses. All the shades were tightly drawn. He unlocked the door and stepped inside where he turned on a dim overhead light. As she followed him, she saw that the first-floor interior was one big open space. As he'd said, it was filled with antiques. Victorian sofas, chests of drawers, marble statues and even a horse watering trough.

He crossed the room, heading for a stairway at the back. They climbed to a second level that was much like the first. The third floor was set up like a loft with a kitchen on one side, a living area and a bedroom in the back. He'd said it was an occasional residence. Anybody else would have been glad to call the place home.

She sank onto the sofa, hugging her knees as she watched Jake standing uneasily a few feet away. After he had come to her rescue, they'd been intent on getting to safety. Now that they were alone together, it seemed everything had changed.

As she watched him standing awkwardly in the living area, she asked, "Sorry you brought me here?"

"No."

"Your face says otherwise. You look like you're going to fly apart with tension."

"I'm thinking about the guy who barged in on you. How did he know you knew Evelyn?"

"He said my name was in her daybook."

"That solves one mystery."

"But you're thinking about us, too."

"Okay. Yeah."

She swallowed. She'd been avoiding Jake Harper because of what she'd sensed between them. Maybe that had been the wrong approach.

"You might as well sit down," she said.

He waited a moment, then took the gun from the waistband of his pants and set it on the table before lowering himself to the other end of the sofa, still eyeing her.

"What are you thinking now?" she asked as she studied his uncertain expression.

"That I've had a lot of weird experiences in my life, but I've never run into anything like this."

"Which part?"

"The whole deal. Evelyn Morgan. Her murder. The mind-reading stuff."

The mind-reading stuff—which was triggered by touching, as far as she could tell. She felt a strong compulsion to reach out and touch him now—for a lot of reasons—but she thought it would be better to keep her hands to herself. For the time being.

Trying to fill the silence, she said, "I have more experience with psychic…phenomena than you do. Murder, not so much."

He laughed. "Yeah."

"I was afraid to find out what was between us. Maybe that's a mistake."

"Why?"

"Because when the guy was getting ready to handcuff me, I had the strong feeling that you were going to show up to rescue me." She dragged in a breath and let it out. "Well, at least I knew something was going to happen to change the equation. I didn't know for sure that it would be you until I saw you standing in the doorway. Why did you come rushing over to my place?"

He blew out a breath. "I'd been thinking about you all day. I told myself that I should ask you some questions. I guess that was an excuse to see you. On the way to your shop, I felt—" He stopped and shrugged. "I don't know what to call it. Anxious, I guess. Like I knew something bad was going down. Specifically, I was sure you were in trouble."

"Lucky for me." She dragged in a breath and let it out. "Thanks for being honest. Did you ever feel something like that before?"

"I've had hunches that turned out to be right."

"Like what?"

"Sometimes when I'm negotiating, I have a sense of how far the other guy's willing to go."

"That could just be experience."

"When I was a teenager on the streets, I was pretty good at picking places to sleep where I knew I'd be safe."

She nodded, thinking that none of that was exactly evidence. "Did you ever have…mind-to-mind communication with anyone else?"

"No. Did you?"

She shook her head. "Only you. In fact…" She let the sentence trail off.

"Are we going to stick with honesty?"

"It's not that easy. I'm not used to revealing myself."

"Neither am I. But it may be to our advantage."

She dragged in a breath and let it out, wondering what he was going to think of her. "Okay. I've never felt close to anyone. Not my parents. Or anyone I called a friend. I was always alone in a way that made me…sad."

She'd never admitted that to anyone. She wanted to look away, but kept her gaze on him and saw him swallow.

He swallowed hard. "Same with me."

"Why do you think it's true?"

He shrugged. "I don't know why. But I always felt there was something missing. Something I should be able to have but couldn't attain."

"Yes! That's the way I felt. Like there should have been more—but there was no way to reach it."

They were both silent for several moments. When he didn't speak, she said, "Something's going on between us. We hardly know each other and yet we know each other better than anyone else we've ever met."

He nodded.

"We ought to see if we can make it stronger."

He kept his gaze fixed on her. "Why?"

"For starters, for safety."

He considered that and asked, "How?"

She kept her gaze steady. "I think you know. As soon as we touched, we made a connection. It brought you to me when I was in danger."

"And you're thinking that if we get closer, it will strengthen the connection between us and make us both safer?"

"Don't you?"

"I think there are risks as well as benefits."

"What risks?"

"I don't know."

"You've taken risks before. What's different now?"

His gaze turned inward. "When I was a teenager, trying to make it on my own, I had nothing much to lose. I was at the bottom, and there was nowhere to go but up. I took a lot of chances. I mean, living on my own. Dealing with adults who would have no compunction about raping or murdering a boy."

Her insides clutched. "Did—"

"No," he answered quickly.

"You think being successful has made you more cautious?"

"I hate thinking of myself that way." He gave her a direct look. "Your experience is different. You came from a stable middle-class home."

She laughed mirthlessly. "Where my parents didn't approve of their daughter trying to make a living in what they considered a nutty profession."

She kept her gaze on him, thinking that this was a strange conversation but that both of them were using it as a way to postpone action.

"So you're willing to take chances. But not with a woman?" she asked.

Chapter Five

The comment had been a calculated risk.

Jake's expression darkened, and Rachel knew she'd insulted a man who prided himself on his courage.

And he wasn't going to let the remark go. His eyes glittered dangerously, making her want to spring off the couch, but she stayed where she was as he slid across the space that separated them and reached for her.

She let her head drop to his shoulder, closed her eyes and held on to him. It was a unique experience. As his arms came up to enfold her, she felt such a confusing rush of emotions that she could hardly cope with them.

Safety was part of it. She was safe in his arms. Along with that came the most overwhelming sexual need she had ever experienced. But she knew that was only one component. She was also keenly aware of the danger simmering below the surface.

It came from the situation they were in. And also the intimacy.

Why? he asked.

I don't know.

Besides the word he had spoken in her mind, she could read the emotions churning within him just as clearly as her own needs and doubts.

If we go any further, there's no going back, he warned.

She didn't have to ask how he knew that. It was as clear to her as it was to him.

Her answer didn't come in words. She lifted her head, staring at him, letting him make the final decision.

He did, lowering his mouth to hers, rubbing his lips gently against hers. It was only a light touch but it sent heat shimmering over her nerve endings. Beaded her nipples to tight points of sensation.

With any other lover, there had always been the question of how fast to go.

In terms of days and hours, she and Jake Harper still hardly knew each other, but in this case, time was the least important factor.

She had confessed her inability to connect with anyone on a deep level. He had said the same thing.

Not now.

When he lifted a hand, brushed it lightly over the swell of her breast, it felt right.

His touch sent heat shooting downward through her body as wayward thoughts shimmered through her brain. Memories that he would rather her not know. Yet he had no way to hide them.

She gasped. *A junkie almost killed you.*

He didn't speak, but she saw him clawing his way out of the man's clutches, then striking back with fists and feet.

As she was absorbing that, another long-ago scene leaped into her mind. A well-dressed man trying to pick up the good-looking boy. Offering money if Jake would come home with him.

She felt the clogging sensation in his throat as he'd backed away and run.

Next she watched him taking a valuable pitcher to a flea market and having a dealer knock it off a table—only to blame the clumsy kid.

I got back at him a few years later by scoring a whole houseload of goods that he'd thought were going to be his.

But it wasn't one-way communication. If his mind was open to her, hers was to him. Her life hadn't been as shocking, but it hadn't been wonderful, either.

She saw herself again in sixth grade, trying to explain why she'd done so well on a book report. And Jake was right along with her, eavesdropping on the memories.

The teacher thought you cheated.

I didn't.

I know. You were so upset.

She tried to pull away from the aftermath, when she'd closed herself in her room, weeping with impotent indignation, but she couldn't shut off the memory until the scene had run its course.

She was open and vulnerable in a way she had never been before.

And while she was so unguarded, she wanted him to know something.

I didn't have anything to do with Evelyn's death.

I know. I think I was using that as an excuse to put distance between us.

Thank you for admitting that.

She had never been so certain of another person's truthfulness, and she knew it was the same for him, too.

The physical contact, the arousal opened the gate between his mind and hers in a way she had never imagined. Not with anyone.

She had been afraid. The fear receded because she knew that he wanted her to trust him. More than he wanted to make love with her. That knowledge made her heart squeeze. He was a tough guy on the outside. But inside…she knew him better than anyone else in the world, because it was impossible to hide the tender core of his soul that he was afraid to reveal.

She wanted him to know how much that meant to her, but she didn't have to tell him. The knowledge was there for his taking. His alone.

When he wrapped his arms around her and leaned back on the sofa, she came with him, sprawling on top of him the way she had in his office. Last time she'd been fighting what she felt. Now she was free to admit she loved the way the length of her body fit against his, starting with the way her breasts molded against his broad chest and moving downward to the erection wedged against her middle.

She let herself feel it and at the same time reached out to know what it was like. For him.

She felt the pleasure radiating from that part of his body as it filled with blood and became hard, the pressure building toward an explosion.

"That's how it is for a man," she murmured, knowing he was doing the same thing, tapping into the sensations of her woman's body. Secret sensations that she didn't know how to describe.

Tingly, he supplied. *Needy. Ripe.*

Ripe! That's a guy word.

She smiled as she said it, with her lips and inside her mind.

He stroked one hand down her body, pressing her closer as he cupped his other hand around the back of her head and brought her mouth to his, lightly at first and then with more urgency.

Urgency they shared.

Never before. Never like this.

I know.

She made a small sound as he deepened the contact, and she drank in the masculine taste of him.

Her mind and body were flooded with sensuality. And something else. Pressure that bordered on pain in her head.

"It's not all good," she whispered.

"It will be."

A man's response. He shifted them to their sides, then cupped his hand around her breast, rubbing his thumb back and forth across the hardened nipple.

Not like this. I want to make love with you for the first time in a bed.

Where?

At the back of the loft.

Her head was pounding, the pain competing with her arousal.

She wanted to tell him to slow down. Or was that what she really wanted?

He climbed to his feet and helped her up. It was dark in the room now, and she felt disoriented.

Of course, he knew that.

"I'll turn on the light."

He crossed the room and flipped the switch.

"Hold it right there," a rough voice said.

She whirled to confront the man who had been in her shop. The man Jake had knocked out. The last time she'd seen him, he'd been lying unconscious on the floor. Then he'd managed to get free and disappear, leaving a pool of blood behind.

Had he hidden outside and followed them here? However he'd found them, he stood in the doorway, a gun in his hand.

It was hard to think over the pounding in her head. The pain was worse than it had been moments ago.

"Now I've got you both, and you're going to be very sorry you messed with me," he said.

Cold fear was like a glacier in the pit of Rachel's stomach. This man had already tried to handcuff her. Then Jake had come in and hit him over the head. Now he was back and roaring mad.

The guy kept his distance, looking from Rachel to Jake and back again. He picked up the gun Jake had left on the table and put it in his own waistband, but somehow he'd acquired a second weapon.

She stood where she was, desperately trying to contact Jake the way they'd done before. Maybe together they could do something. A few minutes ago they'd been inside each other's minds, but they'd been touching intimately and she was sure that had made the difference.

They were separated by nine feet of space, and there was no way she could achieve the kind of contact that they'd had on the sofa.

She saw the strained expression on his face and knew he was trying to reach out to her. But it seemed he couldn't do it, either. His thoughts just weren't available to her. Maybe the headache had wiped the ability away.

"We're not taking any chances," the man with the gun said. "First you're going to tie up your lover boy. Then I'll cuff you, and he can watch the questioning."

"Stay the hell away from her!" Jake growled.

"I don't think you can do much about it, smart guy."

He looked around the room and spotted a table and two wooden chairs.

"Pull out one of the chairs," he said to Jake. "And sit down so your girlfriend can tie you up. Move slowly, and don't try anything tricky."

As a sliver of hope bloomed inside Rachel, she struggled to keep her face a mask of fear. If she and Jake were going to do anything…mental to get away, they'd have to be touching, and their captor had just given them the opportunity to do that.

Jake was still glaring at the guy, but Rachel had come to know him very well, and she sensed the defiance in his eyes.

The guy had a coil of rope under his jacket. He tossed it toward Rachel. When it landed on the floor, she stood staring at it as if she was afraid of what was coming next.

She *was* afraid, but not for the reason he assumed.

"Pick it up!"

She bent and picked up the rope, then walked stiff-legged toward Jake.

"Tie his hands behind him. And no playing around this time. Or I *will* shoot."

She made a sound of protest, then walked in back of Jake, who slung his hands behind him.

Kneeling, she grabbed his wrist. For a moment nothing happened, and she worried she was too frightened to activate the link between them.

Then she heard his voice in her head.

Rachel!

Thank God. What are we going to do?

Work together.

"Don't just kneel there. Tie him up," the guy ordered in a grating voice.

She wound some of the rope around Jake's right wrist, striving to keep the connection with him when her heart was pounding so hard that she could barely think.

She caught a mental picture that she knew wasn't her own thought. A picture of the man rushing across the room and smashing his head into the window. It was so vivid that she glanced up to make sure the guy was still holding the gun on them.

Help me.

I don't know how.

Neither do I, but we have to get that picture into his mind. Unless you've got a better idea.

She didn't.

Bending her head so her face didn't show, she pretended to work on tying Jake.

Help me send him the picture.

How? I don't know!

She caught the frustration in Jake's inner voice.

Just see it the way I'm seeing it and blast it toward him. Like you're throwing a baseball.

Was there a hope in heaven of that working? It had to! Because once they were restrained, the man with the gun could do whatever he wanted to them.

She had never tried to do anything like what Jake was asking. Not in her life. But she did her best to follow his lead. It was like feeling around in the dark looking for a needle she'd dropped on the floor, and she had no idea where it was.

When she made a frustrated sound, he answered, *It's our only chance.*

The mental warning galvanized her. They had to get away from this guy, or he was going to do something horrible—to both of them. As he'd done to Evelyn.

She thrust that terrible thought from her mind. All that mattered was getting away, and Jake had given them a way to do it, if they could pull it off.

With every shred of will she possessed, she focused on the picture Jake had given her—of the man rushing across the room and slamming his head into the window. At the same time, as she drilled the picture into her brain cells, she tried to aim it toward their captor.

When she dared to glance up, she saw that his face had turned pale. At least he must be getting the image. But was he going to act on it?

Everything you've got, Jake whispered in her mind, and she felt the resolve pouring out of him. She could see drops of moisture on the back of his neck as he strained to do the impossible.

No, not impossible, because they were doing it.

"Quit stalling," the guy said, but his voice had taken on a strangled quality.

Because she knew he couldn't see what she was doing, she stopped working with the rope so that her total attention was on the mental mission.

The gunman looked toward the window, then back at Jake.

"What…are you doing?" he asked.

"Nothing."

"You're putting thoughts in my head."

"How could I do that?"

"I don't know." He raised the gun. "Stop it. Stop it right now or you're going to be missing a kneecap."

Fear leaped inside Rachel, and she lost her focus.

The guy's expression changed. Suddenly he looked more confident. Addressing her, he said, "Finish what you're doing."

"I will," she whispered through gritted teeth as her resolve strengthened. Jake was right. They could do this—because they had to.

Grimly, she poured her will into the picture that Jake had conjured up.

The guy looked from them to the window again. Then he steadied the gun on Jake.

"It's you. You're doing this."

In that terrible moment, Rachel knew he was going to pull the trigger.

Chapter Six

Desperate to get Jake out of the line of fire, Rachel pushed the chair over.

He had caught her intention and rolled away as he hit the floor. She went down, too, sprawling on the rug.

But the gun followed Jake.

Rachel struggled with every shred of resolve to make the man aim away.

The window image. The window, Jake shouted in her head.

She was torn, but she did what he asked.

In the next second, the man swung the gun toward the window and fired. She goggled at the unexpected response, but he was already running toward the shattered glass. He crashed against it, screaming as shards tore into his flesh.

Jake scrambled up, charging after the guy, but he was already through the window. They were on the third story, but he fell only half a story—to the roof at the back of the next building.

Rachel saw him hit the roof, then right himself. The gun was still in his hand. Cursing as he turned back toward them, he started to fire, but Jake had already pulled her away and pushed her to the floor.

A stream of bullets whizzed over their heads.

"Stay low."

They crawled across the floor, toward the opposite side of the room.

"Grab your bag."

Her bag. She'd forgotten that she'd packed some clothing only an hour before. That seemed like a thousand years ago. Getting out of here alive was the important point, but she grabbed the bag as she passed.

The shooting had stopped.

"He could have gone around front," Jake whispered as they reached the ground floor.

In the distance she could hear the wail of a siren. Apparently someone had called the police in response to the gunfire.

"But I'm guessing he won't wait around for the cops," Jake added.

Still, he peered cautiously around the door frame before stepping out.

"Come on."

"Where?"

"Away from here."

He led her down the street at a trot. They'd just turned a corner when patrol cars with flashing lights pulled up in front of his building. Uniformed officers leaped out and charged the door.

"Police. Open up."

When no one answered, they rammed the door open.

Rachel winced. "What about all those antiques?"

"I'll get my assistant, Patrick, to secure the place later. Meanwhile, we'd better get out of the area," Jake muttered, ushering her down an alley.

"We still don't know who that guy is," Rachel said as she trotted alongside him.

"We'll find out. We can call him by his fake name, Eric Smithson, for now."

"How did you think of the window thing?"

"I don't know. It just came to me while I was staring down the muzzle of his gun. I figured that getting him focused on hurting himself was the only way we could escape."

She glanced at Jake, then away.

"I didn't know we could do anything like that. I didn't know *anybody* could do it."

"Neither did I. We almost couldn't, even with the connection we've got." He turned toward her. "We have to strengthen the bond between us. Make it more certain so that we can count on it when we need it."

Rachel was still trying to process what had happened.

"Was he watching us?" she asked, hearing her voice go high and thin.

"You mean on the sofa?"

"Yes."

"Probably. Does it matter?"

"I'm embarrassed."

"He almost killed us and you're embarrassed about being seen making out?"

"It was…private."

They were several blocks away. Jake stopped walking and backed into the shadows, pulling her with him. She came willingly into his arms. The heat that had flared between them blazed up as he brought his mouth down on hers for a hot, frantic kiss that celebrated their escape and promised to take up where they'd left off.

She let her mind open to him. Let him see all the fear that she'd pushed aside.

You were very brave.

Did I have a choice?

Not if we wanted to escape. Speaking of which, I think we'd better get out of the city.

I think that's right.

He kept her hand in his as he started walking again, the pleasant buzz of connection simmering between them. Not the headache, thank the Lord. She remembered a trace of it from their first touch. Now it only seemed to come when they were on the verge of real intimacy, when the mental images were coming fast and furious.

They turned into an alley with rows of garages. As she looked at them, she knew where he was going to stop.

"I guess we're not stealing a car," she said as the picture of a late-model Mercedes filled her mind. It was Jake's.

"I have vehicles in several locations around the Quarter." He gestured toward the garage door. "This one's kind of a tight fit. Let me drive out before you get in."

He pulled the car into the alley, then used the remote control to close the door behind him.

When she joined him in the front seat, she leaned her head back and closed her eyes, but she couldn't stop a heated scene from flickering in her mind. He was thinking about pushing back his seat, pulling her into his lap, making love to her right there.

Guy thoughts.

"This mind-reading stuff is a little inconvenient," he muttered.

She laughed. "I guess we'll have to work on—" she raised her shoulder "—a shield."

"How?"

"Do I know?"

He pulled out of the alley and headed across the river into Orleans Parish. Classic rock was playing on the radio. One of the Creedence Clearwater Revival tunes she liked. She was letting the music distract her, when the song stopped abruptly.

"We interrupt our regular programming with an announcement from the New Orleans police concerning a pair of fugitives—Jake Harper and Rachel Gregory. Harper is a

New Orleans businessman. Gregory is a French Quarter tarot card reader."

"Fugitives?" she gasped.

"Wanted for questioning concerning a murder at the Bourbon Arms Hotel yesterday. Earlier this evening they apparently participated in a shoot-out at a warehouse owned by Harper."

Jake cursed under his breath.

Rachel struggled to drag air into her lungs. "They think we killed Evelyn Morgan? But we weren't even there."

"They didn't exactly go that far. We're wanted for questioning."

"But why?"

"The guy could have left some evidence that makes the cops think we're involved."

Her voice rose in outrage as she continued, "Then he shoots up your warehouse, and that's our fault, too?"

"I'd say he's done this kind of thing before and he knows what strings to pull."

"A real pro." She clenched her fingers on the armrest. "So he's still after us. And we can't go to the police for help because he's framed us."

"I think we already agreed not to get the police involved."

"That was before he attacked us a second time."

Jake sighed. "We've got to figure out who he is and why he came after us. And who Evelyn Morgan is really."

He slowed when he reached the outskirts of a small town and pulled into the parking lot of a fast-food restaurant. "What are you doing?"

"Making a call."

"Is it safe?"

"If I keep it short, I think so. I need to talk to my assistant."

A man picked up on the first ring, and his voice was loud enough for Rachel to hear.

"Jake! The cops are after you. It's on the news."

"I know. I didn't do it." He laughed. "Well, they all say that, but in this case, it's true."

"Where are you?"

"Better not say."

"Yeah. Right. What do you want me to do?"

"Keep things running smoothly until I get back."

"Of course."

"And cooperate with the cops. If they want to search my office, let them. I don't have anything to hide."

"Okay."

"Next time I call you, you won't recognize the number."

"Take care of yourself."

"I will." He hung up, switched off the phone, then hesitated.

"Are you wondering if you should crush it?" she asked.

He nodded.

"I think they can't trace it if you keep it off."

"How do you know?"

"Spy novels."

He snorted, then gave her a considering look. "You okay?" he asked.

"Not really."

"We will be."

"You promise?"

"Yes."

He kept driving, using a secondary road that took them farther from the city.

Finally, in a town about fifty miles from home, he came to a commercial strip with several motels. After driving past the big chains, he stopped at a smaller establishment.

"What about this?"

"Kind of run-down."

"I'm sorry. I'd like to have found a nicer place, but this is probably the safest."

When he parked a dozen yards from the lobby, she clenched her fingers on his arm. "What if the cops come here?"

"I think I can minimize the risk."

He climbed out of the car and came back carrying an overnight bag. After slipping behind the wheel again, he opened the bag and took out a baseball cap, which he pulled down so the visor partly hid his face.

"That's going to make a difference?"

"Best I can do with my looks on short notice, but I'm going to tell the desk clerk a story that will throw him off."

"Like what?"

He sighed. "I'm fooling around with a married woman, and I'm willing to pay for anonymity."

"Thanks."

When she dipped into his head again, she got confirmation of that. He was thinking he wouldn't have any trouble convincing the clerk he was here for sex. *Another guy thought.*

Sorry. Changing the subject, he said, "Naturally a man in that position would pay in cash."

"Oh, Lord, I didn't even think about that. We can't use a credit card, right?"

"Well, not in your name or mine."

"You have an alternate?"

"Yeah."

"Why?"

He shrugged. "I've gotten into some scrapes from time to time. It seemed prudent to be prepared."

"You're supposed to be a legitimate businessman. Not a criminal."

"Let's not get too far into that discussion."

"I can find out—from your mind."

"Yes, you can." He sighed. "Okay. I was having a dispute with some business associates who weren't too fussy about their methods. I figured that if I had to go underground to keep from getting blown away, I'd better be prepared."

It wasn't a detailed explanation, but she got the drift.

"I'll go in alone. You stay here, and kind of slip down in your seat like you're worried the husband might spot you. Okay?"

JAKE COULD SEE SHE WASN'T okay, but she gave her agreement. He left the bag in the driver's seat, and before he reached the door, he looked back at Rachel. She had slid lower in the seat, but he knew she was watching him.

She was from a much different background than his. Making up stories didn't come easily to her, but she was adapting very well to the life they were leading at the moment.

What about in the future? He tried not to think about that. Could he keep it out of his mind when he touched her again? He couldn't say. He only knew he felt as if he was in a huge truck, rushing to some dangerous destination. The brakes had failed, and he was trying with all his strength to keep the rig from plunging off a mountain and smashing on the jagged rocks below.

He didn't think that was too much of an exaggeration for the present situation. A lot of stuff was going down. In a very short span of time.

He and Rachel were in danger, and not just from the cops or the guy who had found them twice in less than an hour. All of which was bad enough, if you considered normal scenarios. But there was another factor, as well. He and Rachel were on the brink of what she'd called mind control, which was either going to save their lives or fry their brains.

He wasn't certain how he knew that, but he was pretty

sure it was true. Maybe from the headache that had tinged his pleasure when they were headed for the bedroom.

He cut off those thoughts as he strode into the motel office. It had appeared empty, but a guy popped up from behind the counter. He looked to be in his mid-twenties, with a wiry build and narrow shoulders. He was wearing a plaid shirt and jeans, and Jake would bet he'd been taking a nap in his chair.

"Help you?"

"I hope so." Jake cleared his throat. "My lady friend and I need a room for the night. Trouble is, her husband is starting to wonder where she's been disappearing in the evenings."

The clerk nodded.

"He could be out looking for us. Or he could have...you know...gotten some friends in the cop department to beat the bushes for us."

"Uh-huh."

"If anybody comes around asking questions, I'd appreciate your keeping your mouth shut about it."

When the guy looked at him expectantly, Jake got out a roll of bills and peeled off a hundred. "If somebody does show up lookin' for us, could you give me a heads-up after they leave the office?"

"Sure thing."

"Do you have a room around back?"

"Yup." He turned and detached a door key off the hook. It was to room fifteen.

Jake took the key and signed the register as John Smith. He wrote down a license number at random and strode back to the car where Rachel was waiting.

"You told your nasty little story?"

"Yes. Better than saying we're a pair of murderers."

"There's that."

He drove around the back of the motel and they both got

out. When he unlocked the door and stepped inside, she followed.

It was a pretty minimal place, but no worse than he had expected. There was a double bed. A beat-up dresser with an old TV. A sagging chair. A small bathroom.

He looked at Rachel, sensing her uncertainty.

"Sorry," he said.

"None of this is your fault."

"Or yours."

She swallowed. "Back before Evelyn Morgan came in for that reading, I thought I knew what I was doing. I mean, my life had run along familiar lines for years, and I was happy with the way things were going, at least as far as my business was concerned."

"Were you really happy or did you tell yourself you were?"

"I was as happy as I could be."

"And now?"

"I've leaped into the unknown."

She laid her hand on his arm, and he knew she was thinking they were wound up in a situation that they still didn't understand—except that they were being chased by a murderer and the cops. But that was only part of it. They still had to deal with whatever was happening on a very personal level.

"Sealing the connection between us is our best shot. Or maybe if we go any further, we blow our brains out. I don't mean with a gun," she said in a strangled voice.

He had been thinking something similar. They were walking a fine line between passion and destruction.

"How do we…do it?" she asked.

He laughed. "The usual way."

Knowing he had reached the limit of his endurance, he hauled her into his arms.

She gasped at the contact, gasped again when he wrapped his arms around her and dragged her tight against his body.

She didn't try to pull away. They both knew it was too late for that. Instead she clung to him with a desperation that echoed his own.

Again, it wasn't simply a guess about what she was feeling. He *knew*.

They swayed together in the center of the little room, and when his hands began to move over her back and shoulders, she did the same, touching him, increasing the contact.

He was so hot now that he thought he might explode, but he wouldn't rush this. He wanted to draw out the pleasure of making love with her for the first time, and he also knew that rushing could be a fatal mistake.

So they touched and murmured unnecessary words to each other because there was nothing they could say that the other didn't sense.

THE MESSAGE CAME TO MICKEY loud and clear from Tanya's mind to his.

We're going to New Orleans.

Why?

First I was thinking about the dead lady. Evelyn Morgan. Now I know something's changed. And it's got to do with us.

She's dead. She can't hurt us.

But someone else can, and we've got to get rid of them.

She must have felt his resistance, because she gave him a stern look.

Mickey tried to make her understand the panic he was feeling. *We have a good thing going. I don't want to mess it up by...sticking our noses in where they don't belong. Why can't we just stay in Baltimore and keep out of it? We can go anywhere else in the country we want. We could even go to France.*

Neither one of us can speak French.

Well, what about Canada?

Too dangerous. Can't you feel it?

He swallowed. He wanted to ignore the gnawing sensations of danger that had him waking up in the middle of the night.

Someone else is about to get the power.

Maybe not. And what if they do? We don't have to get anywhere near them.

Suppose they come after us?

Why would they?

Because they know it's either us or them, and we have to stop them before they get...complete control.

She went silent, and he could feel her sending her mind out toward the other ones. The man and woman who were like him and Tanya.

He didn't know why it had happened to them. The mind-meld thing. He didn't know why it had happened to anyone else, either.

Maybe they'll blow their brains out. Like we almost did.

We can hope.

We don't have to go after them, he said again without much conviction. She was the one who made the major decisions, and he knew that they would be heading south if the other couple survived.

WHEN THEY'D GOTTEN CLOSE before, Jake had picked up impressions of Rachel's past. And she of his. Now they were both focused on this moment in time. The two of them. Alone in a room. Where nobody could interrupt them.

We hope.

We're all right, he assured her, praying it was true. And she caught that, too.

You can't lie to me.

I was trying to reassure you.

You can't do that, either. Not really.

Because he hated hearing her say that, he lowered his mouth to hers for a kiss that would have silenced her words. It couldn't silence her thoughts, but he knew she was doing the same thing he was. Focusing on the two of them. Arousing each other. Getting ready to take a step that would change everything.

Everything's already changed.

That was true, too.

His head was pounding. A background beat that he didn't like.

But that was part of the whole thing.

The first time a woman makes love, there's pain.

Not a headache. Despite himself, he laughed. And she did, too.

Maybe we have to break through a barrier, get tuned to each other.

How?

Only one way.

A man's answer.

She made the wry observation, but he knew they were on the same wavelength.

Their clothing was in the way. He worked her shirt out of her waistband and slipped his hands under, sighing as he stroked the soft skin of her back.

Then he reached up to unhook her bra so that he could slide his hands to her front and cup her breasts.

"Oh."

He smiled as he kissed her. He wanted to make her so hot that she couldn't think straight. Maybe that was the way to wipe out the pain building inside his skull.

He knew she caught that thought when she slid her hand

down the front of his body, cupping her fingers over his erection, rocking her palm against him.

Not too much of that. I want this to last.

She raised her hands, doing what he had done, slipping her fingers under his T-shirt so that she could stroke his back before pushing the fabric up.

He stepped away from her and pulled the shirt over his head.

She unbuttoned her shirt and tossed it away along with her bra.

He stared at her in the dim light coming through the Venetian blinds. "You are so beautiful."

She grinned. "You've got a pretty nice chest, too."

He crossed to the window and pulled the cord, closing the blinds. Then he walked to the bathroom and turned on the light, closing the door partway so that there was only a dim glow in the bedroom.

When he looked back to her, he saw that she had turned down the covers and was reaching for the snap at the top of her slacks.

"Let me."

She went still as he crossed to her, worked the snap, then slowly lowered the zipper so that he could reach his hand inside her slacks and inside her panties, combing his fingers through the crinkly hair at the juncture of her legs.

He felt so much. Too much. Sexual arousal, the thoughts leaping toward him—and the pounding in his head that might wipe out everything else.

He strove to put that worry out of his mind. It wouldn't happen if they did this right.

Which was what, exactly?

As he caressed her, he moved his lips against hers, stroking then nibbling with his teeth. He knew the exact amount of pressure that would bring her pleasure instead of pain because he could follow her reaction to the sensations.

A firestorm of heat threatened to overwhelm him.

If he didn't make love with her...

He couldn't finish the thought because the idea of stopping had become unbearable. Worse than the pounding in his head. He would die if he didn't make love to Rachel.

And die if he did?

He sensed her fear, and he knew she sensed his in equal measure.

He thought of the tried-and-true male line about not being able to stop. It was a lie. He could always stop.

Until this moment.

They staggered together to the bed and flopped onto the mattress. He rolled toward her, gathering her close, his body rocking against hers.

When it registered that neither one of them had taken off their pants, he groaned.

Her laughter rang in his head as they rolled away from each other, each shedding the remainder of their clothing.

When they were both naked, he reached for her again, both of them gasping at the sensation of skin against skin.

They were trembling, coping with more than any individual should have to bear alone. His head throbbed, and he knew that he might stroke out from the intensity.

He heard her gasp. Not just the sound, but in his mind—generated by the same pain he felt.

If he let her go, would it stop? Or would snapping the connection now finish them off?

Maybe that was the key to survival. The courage to see this through—no matter where it led.

The only path is forward.

Together.

We aren't alone, she answered.

Still, it was hard to hold on to that truth in any rational way. Needing to be closer to her, he slid his hand down her body again, dipping into her folds, finding her wet and molten for him. He didn't have to ask if she was ready to take the final step. He knew.

Yes!

And she didn't have to use her hand to guide him into her. They simply did it, moving from separate individuals to one being in a smooth, sure motion.

He was inside her. Or was she inside him? He didn't know anymore where he ended and she began. He only knew that every sense was tuned to her. Every thought. And she to him.

One of them began to move. No, it was both of them, because the pressure in their brains was too great, and the only way to relieve it was through sexual climax.

That didn't make sense. Yet he thought it was true, at least with the part of his mind that could still function coherently.

Or was it simply instinct that had him grasping for completion, desperate to finish this—and bring her along with him, because if it didn't end soon, he knew he would die.

None of it made sense. But he was beyond trying to understand what was happening. He could only focus on the wonderful sensations—his and hers—as they rushed toward ecstasy…or death.

He couldn't have stopped now if the door had burst open and the man with the gun had come charging in firing at point-blank range.

He clung to Rachel and she to him. Not just with his hands, with his mind. It was everything. What he had sought his whole life. Yet as he hovered on the edge of a blinding explosion, he wasn't sure he would survive.

Chapter Seven

You must. We must.
   I'm lost without you.
   Was that true?
   It felt like the truth to Jake.
   They crashed through a barrier that seemed to transcend time and space, the two of them together, always together as climax rocked them, blinding them to everything but what they had found together. They held tightly to each other as they came down to earth again, each of them panting, each of them marveling at what they had done together.
   In that moment, there was nothing he could hide from her. Nothing she could hide from him. He didn't even try, just drifted on the perfect oneness of their shared consciousness.
   Finally, he understood how alone he had been. Alone in a way that he had never been able to admit to anyone, especially himself.
   He had been cut off from ordinary human relationships. Not because he was less, as he'd always thought. It was just the opposite. Because he was more.
   Neither one of us was complete, she whispered in his mind.
   Now we are.
   How did it happen?
   We found each other. We forged a...bond.

It could have killed us. If...

If we had a failure of nerve.

You're too strong for that.

So are you. Neither one of us was going to give up.

He smiled, thinking about her strength—and his. Rolling to his side, he took her with him, feeling more peaceful than he ever had in his life.

You need to sleep.

So do you.

I don't want to lose this.

I'll be here when you wake up. I'll always be here.

Content, they drifted off, each of them needing to recharge the energy they had expended.

Sometime later, Jake woke, and she did, too. At the same time.

He eased far enough away to switch on the bedside lamp, then blinked in the sudden glow.

Raising himself on his elbow, he smiled down at Rachel.

"Would you have believed that could happen—if anyone had told you?"

"No."

"We've found something nobody else has."

"Maybe somebody," she answered.

"Who?"

"People like us."

Who would that be? he asked himself.

"Maybe Evelyn Morgan came to town to give us a heads-up."

Some of the conversation was spoken, some was in their minds. It didn't matter which as they lay there in bed, curled together.

She nodded gravely. "And now she's dead."

"And we have to figure out what she wanted to tell us."

Isn't this enough?

You know it isn't. That guy's still after us. And the cops.

She winced. "I'd kind of pushed that to the back of my mind."

"So did I. Which was good, because we needed to focus on each other."

To keep our heads from exploding, she clarified.

A nice way to put it, but yeah.

It was your thought.

"This isn't productive," he finally said. *We have to find out what Evelyn Morgan wanted to tell us.*

He could feel her thinking—and when an idea came into her head, he didn't have to ask what it was.

Still, she said it aloud, maybe to test it. "The tarot deck she handled is in my shop. If I do a reading with it, maybe I can get more insight into what she wanted."

"Kind of dangerous going back there."

She ignored the observation and went on. "But we need clues. We can't just keep running."

He sighed. "All right. But not until tomorrow."

She laughed. "I think I know why. You want to find out if making love is going to give us a headache again."

"I don't think it will. Like what you said about a woman's virginity. The first time has unpleasant aspects. But you're right. We'd better find out."

RACHEL WOKE AND FELT A moment of disorientation. Then she felt Jake lying next to her. Not just his body but his mind, so open and vulnerable to her that she could barely breathe.

I know, his voice echoed in her head as he reached for her. She came into his arms.

Like coming home.

To a life I never knew.

They basked in the wonder of it as they began to kiss and stroke each other. A couple making lazy love in the morning. Only it was so much more. They were strengthening the link between them.

Finally, the need for fuel drove them from the motel. They were both feeling wonderful. Yet she knew they were both unsettled, as well.

Jake squeezed her hand.

Be careful what you wish for.

Are you sorry?

Of course not, he answered.

But she knew it wasn't entirely true. The lack of mental privacy was too much a part of the equation.

We'll figure out how to deal with it.

We hope.

If that guy doesn't get us.

He won't.

She wanted to cling to Jake's reassurance. But the man who kept finding them seemed to have superhuman powers, at least with regard to getting up and walking away from injuries that would have landed anyone else in the hospital.

Jake pulled his hand away, lessening the mental connection between them.

When they passed a pancake house, she wanted to stop.

Sorry. Too public.

I know.

They settled for a quick breakfast from the drive-through of a fast-food restaurant.

"Forget the pancake place," Jake muttered. "We should be celebrating at a special breakfast. Maybe at Brennan's."

She smiled at him as she took in the mental picture he was projecting. The two of them at an elegantly set table, sipping mimosas as they waited for their orders of eggs Benedict.

We've got plenty of time for that.

But this is our only first morning after.

She laid her hand over his. There was nothing either of

them could say that the other wasn't thinking. It should have been a magical time for them. Instead, they were dodging a killer—and the cops. And they didn't even know what the killer was after. Something to do with Evelyn Morgan. But what?

Jake stayed under the speed limit on the way back to town, and they both kept an eye out for patrol officers who might be looking for the man-and-woman murder team.

"What do you think they found at the crime scene that pointed back to us?" she asked. "I mean, it might not be evidence the guy planted at all."

"We both touched her."

"You mean, we left DNA? I don't think it works that way."

"Well, let's go low-tech. Maybe she had both our phone numbers and addresses with her. That might do it. Maybe she wrote something down about us, and the cops have the information."

"That guy said he got my name from her daybook. Does that mean he didn't take it?"

"If he wanted to frame us, that would be a smart move."

"Yes," she murmured. "And then there was a smashed window and a gunfight in the apartment over your warehouse." She sighed. "I guess it's lucky we didn't stick around to make a police report."

He slowed when they entered the city, then took a route to the Garden District.

"Where are we going?"

"To pick up a different vehicle."

"How many do you have?"

"Like I said, several."

They drove into an alley running in back of a row of painted ladies—Victorian mansions that were decked out in multiple colors in the New Orleans tradition. Behind the formal garden of a mauve, green and purple house was a detached garage where Jake exchanged the Mercedes for a blue panel truck with the back and side windows blacked out.

"Do you transport drugs in this thing?" she asked as she transferred her travel bag to the back of the vehicle.

"Actually, I use it to pick up antiques from estate sales. I bought it secondhand and never bothered to put my name on the side."

"Lucky for us."

They turned toward the French Quarter and drove past her shop. The closed sign was still on the door, and there was no one hanging around.

"Would they have stationed an officer inside?" Rachel asked.

"Don't know. But they're probably not expecting us to come back."

"We don't have to go in from the street. We can get into my apartment, then go down the inside stairway we used the other day."

"Good."

"Drive around to the alley. There's a small lot in back of a dress shop a few doors down from my place, but it went out of business."

When they pulled in, Jake asked her to wait while he took a quick look around.

As he stepped out of view, she felt her stomach clench. She might be having trouble coping with being so open to him when they were touching, but having him out of her sight was worse. At least when they were in so much trouble.

When he reappeared, she breathed out a small sigh.

"Looks like the coast is clear."

They climbed up an outside stairway to a second-story balcony, then onto the next roof and over to the back of Rachel's shop. A fire escape led to her apartment.

They climbed again, and she stopped when she came to the window, which was locked.

"Let me have a go at it," Jake said.

When she stepped aside, he started jiggling the frame, and it didn't take too long before the old lock sprang open.

"Nice!" she muttered.

"Sorry. I guess you should get new ones when this is all over."

"If it's ever over."

He opened the window and stepped through into her living room. She followed, seeing him look around at the antiques she'd inherited from her parents and the finds she'd picked up at flea markets. They'd been here before, but they'd been too busy for him to take in the surroundings.

"You have good taste."

"Coming from you, that's a big compliment."

He reached for her, and folded her close. She leaned into him, and they swayed together on the middle of the Oriental rug that she'd found at a garage sale.

"This is hard," she said in a strained voice.

"For a lot of reasons. First of all, things are happening so fast that we can't really absorb them."

She wanted to ask how everything was going to come out. Although she didn't voice the question, she heard his answer.

The way we want it to.

Which means what?

We'll figure it out.

It wasn't exactly what she wanted to hear. But she'd just met him a couple of days ago. What was he supposed to say, that they were going to get married and settle down like a normal couple?

He probably knew what she was thinking, and she silently cursed the relationship that had them joined at the mind.

"We'd better get the cards and get out of here," he said.

"Wait. There's something else." Rachel went to the closet where she kept the things from her parents' house and retrieved the album. After setting it on the dresser, she flipped rapidly to the page with the picture where she was standing with her mother in front of the clinic.

"Have you ever seen this place?" she asked Jake.

He studied the picture. "I don't know. Why?"

"I think it's important."

He didn't bother to ask why as he continued to stare at the photo. "That's you?"

"Yes."

"You were a cute little kid. How old were you there?"

She took in her appearance. "I look like I'm about three."

"I don't remember much from that age."

"Neither do I." She sighed. "I'd like to read the name on the sign, but the letters are blocked by that branch."

"Take the picture with you."

She slipped the photo out of the mountings and slid it into her purse.

"We'd better finish our business here."

Nodding, she led him to the stairs, but he held her back so that he went first.

When he reached the ground floor, he hesitated for a moment before waving her down the stairs.

In the shop, she looked around. The place was as she'd left it, with the overturned chair and the bloodstain still in the middle of the floor—a vivid reminder of their narrow escape.

She shivered as she looked at the blood and the other evidence of their fight with the intruder. The only comment that came to mind was, "You said someone was going to clean it up."

"Slipped my mind. Sorry."

"We've been busy."

He reached for her hand and squeezed, then looked around.

"I don't think the cops have been here yet, but they're going to show up sometime."

"What about Eric Smithson?"

He shrugged.

With her heart pounding, she crossed to the corner where she kept her tarot decks. She had just picked up the one that Evelyn Morgan had handled, when the shop door opened, and she froze, remembering that she hadn't locked it.

When a tough-looking man in a business suit stepped through the door, Jake grabbed her free hand, holding tight while he turned to face the guy.

Rachel's pulse was pounding as she slipped the cards into her purse.

"Who are you?" Jake said as though he had every right to be there and the other guy was trespassing.

"Detective Peter Overly."

Not the same detective Jake had met outside the Bourbon Street Arms.

As the man stared at them, his eyes widened. "What the hell?" He must have been reaching for a gun, but his hand stilled as a look of confusion swept over his face.

Rachel knew what Jake had in mind. As he pressed his shoulder to hers, she added her silent voice to his.

We're just customers. We came in here looking for a reading. You don't recognize us. We aren't the people you're looking for.

"We're just customers looking for Rachel Gregory," Jake said in an even voice.

Overly gave them a hard look. "No, you're—" He stopped, looking even more muddled. "You're…"

"Customers looking for Rachel Gregory," Jake repeated, reinforcing the statement with a mental message. "Sorry to intrude."

The guy wasn't totally ready to buy it.

"How did you get in here?"

"I guess the same way you did. The door wasn't locked."

As he spoke, Jake edged around the detective, heading for the exit. Rachel came with him, her fingers digging into his as she prayed that they could pull this off. They'd gotten Eric Smithson to crash through a window. An act of violence.

This wasn't violent. It should be easier. Except that there was something about this cop that helped him resist them. She didn't know what it was, but it gave her the idea that some people were more susceptible than others.

"You consulted Gregory before?" he asked in a challenging voice.

"No," Jake said.

"Yes," she said. Unfortunately, they were both too focused on the detective to be in sync. He gave them a hard look.

Rachel tried to recover. "I have, but my husband hasn't."

"Why are you here?"

"I persuaded him to try her," Rachel said, both of them still backing away.

"Yes, she sounds like one talented lady," Jake added, spreading it on a little thick.

"Let's see some identification," the detective answered.

"Sorry, we made a mistake," Jake said, still trying to misdirect the guy.

Was this really going to work?

The detective was watching them with narrowed eyes, and Rachel could almost picture his mind trying to sort reality from the fantasy Jake was projecting.

"Come on, honey. I think we showed up at the wrong time," Jake murmured as he led them around the shelf that had fallen over.

They were almost to the door when the detective suddenly straightened and called out, "No! Wait. You're not customers. You're Gregory and Harper. The fugitives. Stop right there."

Chapter Eight

As the detective pulled his gun, they both went rigid.

"Hands in the air."

When they complied, he said, "I didn't think you'd be dumb enough to come back here."

My fault, Rachel silently said.

We'll get out of it.

How?

Put your hand on your forehead. Act like you're going to faint.

Not far from the truth.

Rachel made a moaning sound and swayed.

As the detective looked toward her, Jake leaped forward and gave him a shove, sending him crashing onto a bookcase full of knickknacks that Rachel had on display.

When the gun discharged, Rachel's heart leaped into her throat. But the bullet crashed into the ceiling as small jars, boxes and figurines rained down on the detective.

For good measure, Jake pushed at a wooden display table, sending it toppling onto the man.

Before he could extricate himself, Jake was pulling Rachel out the door.

He charged down the sidewalk, hurrying her along. They turned a corner into an alley, then to the back of the buildings, to the lot where Jake had left the truck.

"Is he following?" Rachel panted.

"I think he was still in the shop when we turned the corner." He looked at her. "Sorry, I think I broke a bunch of your stuff."

"Consider it the cost of doing business."

He made a snorting sound as he started the engine and pulled out of the space, heading down the alley at a reasonable pace, not as though anyone was after them.

Rachel craned her neck around, but she didn't see anyone following, either on foot or in a vehicle. Hopefully, the detective wouldn't even know what they were driving.

"I think we got away," she murmured.

"For now."

"Oh, thanks." She swung her head toward him. "That was clever, though, trying to convince him we were someone else."

"It worked for a few moments."

"Long enough for us to get away."

He sighed. "You mean, with a power assist from a bookcase and a display table."

"We'll get better at it. Maybe you have a particular talent for putting ideas into people's heads."

"I don't think I'll put it on a job application."

She winced. "I wish we could get out of town and hole up somewhere to practice mental skills."

"We can't hole up somewhere. We have to stay here and figure out what's going on. And clear our names."

"You're right," she said, nodding. "I guess I was just wishing that wasn't the case."

She laid her hand over his as they drove, the contact comforting and at the same time unsettling.

She could hear him mentally running through possible scenarios and discarding them.

Let's try the cards, she said. *We went to a lot of trouble to get them.*

Yeah. We'll check into another motel, not the one we chose last time.

Because she needed a little separation, she pulled her hand away and leaned back, closing her eyes as he drove.

"You need to dye your hair," he suddenly said after they'd ridden in silence for a few miles.

"I guess so."

"And I should shave my head."

"No! That will look awful."

He laughed. "You care?"

"You're my handsome devil of a wheeler-dealer."

"Okay. I'll stick with the hat. And change the look of my clothing. You, too."

She nodded. When he came to a discount department store, he slowed and pulled into the parking lot.

"We'll go in separately. And take as little time as possible. I'll get some plaid shirts and jeans."

"Not your look."

"Like I said…" He gave her a considering look. "Stay down while I'm gone."

She slouched into her seat, thinking that being on the run wasn't great for her back.

Jake returned in less than fifteen minutes. In his new clothes he looked nothing like the successful businessman he was and more like a good ol' boy. He tossed a bag in the backseat, then after getting in, he handed her some cash.

She might have protested, but he put his hand on her arm, silently telling her that what he had was hers, too. Which meant what for the future? She might have asked, but she knew neither one of them wanted to look too far ahead.

Before they could get into a mental discussion that was going to make them both uncomfortable, she got out and headed for the store. In the women's department, she bought jeans, a jean jacket and a couple of tops. As she changed in the ladies' dressing room, she tried to keep her mind in neutral. But the reason for the shopping trip came slamming back at her when she went to the health and beauty aids department. She'd never thought of dying her hair before, and when she started reading the directions, all the steps she'd have to take to go blond made her stomach knot.

When she got back to the car, Jake put his hand on her arm.

"Couldn't bring yourself to dye your hair?" he asked, though she knew he'd read the answer in her thoughts.

"Sorry."

He touched a dark curl near her ear. "I didn't like the idea much. You look perfect with dark hair."

"What about leaving it down?"

"Right."

She made the switch as he drove to the other side of town, where they picked up lunch at another fast-food restaurant, then checked into a small motel.

"Did you tell that sleeping-with-a married-woman story again?" she asked when he returned.

"Naw. I just did my good old Southern-boy routine," he said, gesturing toward his downscale outfit.

She knew he was trying to lighten the mood, but it wasn't working. At least not for her.

Inside the room, they sat at the table by the window, and she managed to eat a little of her burger and drink her iced tea before getting out the tarot deck that she'd shoved in her pocket.

He got up and restlessly walked around the room as she shuffled through the deck, finding the cards that Evelyn Morgan had selected for her reading.

Jake came over to the table as she pulled out the Fool and laid it upside down.

"Why is it upside down?" he asked.

"Because I'm laying the cards out the way they were when Evelyn Morgan pulled them."

"It makes a difference?"

"Yes. A lot of cards that you'd want to get in the upright position are much less favorable when turned the other way." She gestured toward the Fool. "Upright, it can point to an adventure. Maybe a new life or a new job or a new relationship." She tapped the card. "Upright, he's full of optimism and hope. He has a clean slate. A fresh start. And maybe that's what Evelyn was looking for when she came to New Orleans. When you turn it the other way, the same desires are expressed, but instead of an adventure, you're likely to get a disaster." She kept her hand on the card. "Look at his satchel. Everything's going to fall out. The sun's setting instead of rising. And the guy looks like he's going to fall off the cliff."

He shrugged.

"You don't look convinced."

"I guess I can see it, when you point it out."

"To me, it's always made sense."

"You're a natural."

She shuffled through the deck again, pulling the Nine of Wands and reversing it, as well.

Jake studied the card, obviously trying to figure out the meaning. "The guy's got a bandage on his head."

"Yes. And he's holding one wand—with eight behind him. It represents the desire to protect and help others. But upside down, it looks like the guy can barely take care of himself."

"How long did it take you to learn all that?"

"Like I said, the basics came easily. But I'm still learning the finer points."

Next she pulled the Hanged Man.

"That looks grim," Jake said.

"It could indicate that she's sorry about her former life and contemplating making sacrifices for the greater good."

"She did end up making a sacrifice—her life."

"I'm guessing that wasn't in her plans."

She pulled more cards, explaining what each meant.

"Are you stalling?" he asked.

"What do you mean?"

"You're going into a lot of detail on all the cards."

She raised her chin, trying to deny his accusation, but the truth was Jake had read her mind. Even without touching her. "Okay, I'm stalling because I'm afraid I'm not going to like what I find out."

"You have to do it anyway," he said, punching out the words.

"I know."

She picked up the cards she'd laid out, sifting them through her hands, trying to get more than she had at the initial reading, but nothing came to her.

"So much for your premonition."

Feeling defeated, she put the cards down and looked up at Jake. "I thought…" She trailed off in frustration.

"Don't beat yourself up."

"I risked us getting arrested by going back to get this particular deck. The one she'd touched."

"Maybe you need a little power assist." Jake walked in back of her and laid his hands on her shoulders.

Like the first time they'd touched, she felt a jolt similar to an electric current going through her, only this time it was familiar, not alarming.

When she sighed, Jake pressed harder, and she caught her breath as she was suddenly assaulted by vivid pictures. Scenes from years ago.

She had expected to get some insight into Evelyn Morgan's life, but this wasn't from the woman who had come to her for a reading. This was something from her own past.

The scene was in a doctor's waiting room.

Not just a doctor's office. A clinic, she answered Jake's mental question because the word leaped into her mind. And all at once she knew more.

The photograph! It's the place from the photograph.

You recognize it?

No, I just know, she answered, feeling a thrill of excitement at the revelation. She'd had no clue where the picture was taken. Now she was seeing it before her.

Where is it? Jake asked.

I know it was a clinic. I still don't know where it was.

Was Evelyn Morgan there?

I don't know, Rachel answered. *But I was.* She saw herself—and other children—playing with an assortment of toys. There was a school bus with wooden figures that fit into holes in the interior. A garage with toy cars. A farm.

Men and women, undoubtedly the parents, sat on chairs and couches around the room. Some were writing on clipboards—probably filling out forms or questionnaires. Others watched their children. There wasn't much conversation among the parents.

"What kind of clinic is it?" Jake probed.

"I don't know. But I went there for tests. The children don't look like they were sick, do they?"

"No."

The strangled sound of his voice jolted her.

"What is it?"

He dragged in a breath and let it out before answering, "I was one of them."

She blinked, struggling to process his words. "Did I hear that right?"

"Yes. I remember it. I was there, too."

She twisted around, and stared at him.

Almost in slow motion, Jake moved his hand down her arm, then to her wrist and finally her hand as he moved around the table, pulled the other chair over and sat down beside her.

She closed her eyes, studying the long-ago scene. She'd forgotten about it, or blocked it out. Now it was so vivid in her mind she felt she could reach out and touch it.

It was as if she was a child again. Back there, where her parents had brought her. And the other children she saw were the same ones, over and over.

"I came there every few months," Jake said in a voice that was full of wonder.

"I did, too."

"And…"

As they sat holding hands, she looked up and saw a boy a few years older watching her. It was Jake, and she gasped in shock. The reaction wasn't from the little girl she'd been. It was from the woman who recognized him.

The little boy scooted over, pushing a school bus full of little peg people. "Wanna play?"

"What's your name?"

"Jake."

"I'm Rachel."

We talked.

Yes.

"I'll be the driver. You be the little girl going to school."

"Okay." She picked up a peg person with brown hair and a red dress.

In the present, Jake's hand tightened on her, but she couldn't take any more. Twisting out of his grasp she jumped up and stood with her shoulders pressed to the door, gasping.

"I'm sorry," she breathed.

"It was a shock—to both of us."

She nodded, her mind desperately trying to sort through new information.

"I'd forgotten all about it," he said.

"So had I."

"Maybe because something disturbing happened there."

Her gaze flew to him. "What?"

"We went there…a lot."

His expression turned hard. "Whatever's happening to us now, I can't believe it doesn't have something to do with that place."

She nodded, unsure and yet certain at the same time.

"You went with your parents?" she asked.

"Yes. Obviously it was before they were killed."

"Then you went into foster care."

"Yeah." He made a rough sound. "Those years were pretty bad. I guess I tried to wipe them out. And anything before, too."

"What happened to your parents?" she asked.

"They died in a fire. My mother threw me out the bedroom window, and somebody caught me."

She winced.

"She saved my life, but not her own."

When she started to speak again, he raised his hand, palm out. "Talking about my childhood after my parents died isn't going to help us figure out what that place was."

"You're right."

"What if they were…doing…some kind of experiments on kids?"

"Like what?"

He shrugged. "I don't have a clue. Psychological testing, maybe."

She found herself following his line of thinking. "Or, you know, there are places that advertise for test subjects and they pay the people they use. What if they were testing some kind of vaccine or drug that turned out to have weird effects on us?"

"And our parents did it for the money?"

"Did your parents need cash?"

"If they did, I was too little to know about it. They died when I was five."

They were both silent, trying to come up with scenarios. But they didn't have enough information. They didn't even know where to find the damn clinic.

"Did you have a good relationship with your parents?" Rachel asked.

"I don't remember."

"I didn't," she whispered.

"In what way?"

"You can probably figure out most of it. I wasn't very close to them. I could spend hours in my own fantasy world. And then...I got interested in psychic stuff. They were down-to-earth people, and what they called mumbo jumbo made them uncomfortable. I went to college early and never really came home again. I hung out around Jackson Square in the summers. After college, I moved in with a group of girls looking for a roommate, but I was never really close to any of them, either."

Her eyes drifted out of focus as she remembered that time.

"My parents hated me hanging around the tarot card readers. They wanted me to get a real job. I just stopped calling them, and they stopped calling me." Her breath hitched. "I didn't even know that my mom was sick until my dad phoned to say she was dead."

He pushed back his chair and strode toward her, taking her in his arms.

They should have told you, so you could visit with her. Maybe make your peace with her.

I disappointed them.

Stop. You couldn't pretend to be something you weren't.

She nodded against his shoulder. She'd gotten up to separate herself from him, but now she held on tight, absorbing the feel of his arms around her—and the soothing thoughts he sent her. It was like nothing she had ever experienced before. Nothing she had ever expected.

Yet she couldn't completely surrender, because that would mean losing herself.

AS JAKE HELD HER, HE caught the thought. He wanted to comfort her, yet he couldn't help feeling a similar resistance to the link that had formed between them. Maybe the resistance was stronger for him than it was for her. He'd been on his own since he was fifteen. Sharing his thoughts and feelings with anyone was entirely new. And it put him on edge.

It's okay to want some privacy, she whispered in his mind.

Are you sure?

Go on.

Slowly, he eased away.

"I'd better call my office." He was grateful for the excuse. "Maybe Patrick can tell me something new."

"You mean, like they caught the killer, and we're off the hook? That would be good, but won't the police…be tracing calls?"

"To be safe, I'll buy a prepaid phone, then throw it away after I check in."

"Good idea."

"We'd better drive to another town, make the call and get out of there."

"How long can we keep paying for rooms—and leaving after a few hours?"

"For a while." He laughed. "If they're not luxury suites."

They left the motel room they'd checked into so recently

and drove for about thirty miles until they came to a commercial area with a drugstore chain. Rachel waited in the car while Jake bought a phone.

Out in the car again, he activated the instrument and punched in the number of his office.

Patrick answered, sounding tentative.

"It's me," Jake said.

"The cops have been all over the place. I'm afraid they've made sort of a mess."

"I'll bet." He dragged in a breath and let it out. "I'm going to be lying low until I figure out how to clear my name."

"You and Rachel Gregory. Is she with you?"

"Let's not talk any longer than we have to."

"Sure. But don't hang up yet. You got a call from a guy who says he's got urgent business with you."

"Oh, yeah?"

Patrick gave him a number.

"And you don't know who he is?" Jake asked.

"Not a clue."

Chapter Nine

Jake wanted to ask more questions, but he knew staying on the line would only make him easier to trace if the cops had his office phone tapped. With a sigh, he ended the call.

"What did he say?" Rachel asked.

"The cops have been searching my office—and probably my house, too."

"And by now they've undoubtedly turned my shop into a wreck. I mean more than we already did with that detective."

"Don't worry about that now." He gestured toward the phone. "Patrick says somebody wants to talk to me."

"Who?"

"The guy didn't give his name."

"It could be the police being tricky." She hitched a breath. "Or that guy who's been after us."

"We'd recognize his voice."

"But what if it's the police?"

"I think I should follow it up. I mean, what if it's someone who knows about Evelyn Morgan—or the clinic?"

"How could they?"

He shrugged, then turned toward her. "If you tell me to forget about it, I will."

"I think we have to," she answered.

"Do you have a bad feeling about it?"

She considered the question. "Maybe. But I'm not in very

good psychic shape. It could just be my general level of anxiety."

He started the engine and turned out of the parking lot, then, in the interest of caution, drove ten miles down the road before pulling into a picnic area. Once again he cut the engine. As he punched in the number, Rachel put her hand on his arm.

They both waited tensely.

A guy picked up on the second ring.

"This is Jake Harper. You wanted to talk to me?"

"Thanks for getting back to me, man."

"Who are you?"

"My name is Mickey."

"And?"

"I have some information that can help you."

"Like what?" Jake asked.

"I'd rather not discuss it over the phone."

Jake's grip tightened on the cell. "You need to be a little more specific."

"About your background."

"That covers a pretty wide area. Give me a hint," Jake said, trying not to sound impatient. He had never met this guy, but he picked up on a strong feeling of dislike.

The man laughed. "Okay. You been having any mental changes recently?"

"Maybe."

"I can tell you some stuff about it. But we got to meet in person."

"Where are you?"

"In New Orleans."

"Do you know the city?"

The man hesitated. "Not so much."

"Okay. There's a warehouse on Burgundy Street." He gave the address. "I'll meet you there at seven."

Before the guy could ask any questions, Jake hung up and sat there, staring through the windshield.

"Who was he, do you think?"

Rachel's question broke into his thoughts. "You heard all that?"

"Yes."

Jake shrugged and looked at her. "Did you pick up anything from him?"

Her brow wrinkled. "It was more what I didn't pick up. I mean, it was like there was a wall between us and him."

Jake nodded. "It came across that way to me, too. There was something...dishonest about him."

"Like he was trying to hide his real intentions."

"Yeah."

"What are we going to do?"

"Meet him."

"That might be dangerous," she pointed out.

"Do we have any choice?" Jake asked. "We're trying to get information, and he may have some. I mean, he mentioned 'mental changes.' Maybe he knows what kind of experiments they were doing at that clinic. And he doesn't want to talk about it over the phone. Not after what happened to Evelyn Morgan."

"That could be right."

"I'll stash you somewhere safe and keep the appointment."

Jake felt Rachel's fingers digging into his arm. "No way are you leaving me hiding someplace while you go off and do something...dangerous."

His stomach clenched. "What if something happens?"

"To you? You don't think that would affect me?"

He nodded tightly. "I guess that's right."

"You *guess?*"

He swallowed hard. "All right, I *know.*"

They were both silent for several moments before she finally said, "We'd better take precautions. Like get there early and be hiding when Mickey arrives."

He smiled. "You're developing your spy skills, I see."

"I'm trying."

"We'd better make it *very* early, in case he has the same idea."

On the way back to town, they discussed some plans, but it quickly became clear that they would have to hang loose.

As they crossed the bridge into New Orleans, they saw a patrol car, and Rachel went rigid.

"Slide down," Jake said, as he'd done on several earlier occasions.

She scrunched low in her seat, but the cop kept going past them.

"How hard are they looking for us?" Rachel asked.

"Let's just say I'd like to minimize the amount of time we stay in the city."

She nodded.

Jake drove around the back of a pawnshop in a neighborhood where Rachel probably wouldn't want to walk around at night by herself. But he was comfortable here.

"What are we doing?" she asked.

"Getting guns."

"I don't want one."

"I do. And I'd feel safer if you're armed, as well."

"Why do we need them? Can't we use…our powers?"

"They're not reliable enough. Don't you remember how it was with that detective at your shop? He was able to resist us."

She nodded tightly.

He could see she didn't like it, but he also knew she saw the wisdom of conventional protection.

The back door to the shop was locked, but Jake had a key.

When they were in the storage area, he turned to Rachel. "Wait here for a moment."

Rachel's nerves were humming. She didn't like being left alone in this place.

When Jake came back and motioned for her to follow, she stepped into a crowded little shop where a wizened, stoop-shouldered coffee-colored man stood behind a display counter.

"I see you're in a mess of trouble," he said, looking Jake up and down.

"We didn't do it."

"I didn't think so. You're capable of a lot of shady stuff, Jake Harper, but not murder, if I'm any judge."

"Thanks for the vote of confidence. Kendall, this is Rachel Gregory. Rachel, this is my friend Kendall Wexler."

"Nice to meet you," they both said.

"She's your partner in crime?"

"We didn't commit any crimes," Jake reiterated, then grimaced, probably when he remembered the incident in her shop with the police detective.

Kendall shuffled from behind the counter to turn the sign from Open to Closed.

As he locked the front door, Rachel looked around. Guitars, banjos and other musical instruments hung on the walls. Display cases were full of everything from laptop computers to sets of flatware, diamond rings and gold beads.

A case behind the counter held an assortment of firearms.

The man swung his gaze to Rachel and smiled. "Could be you hooked up with the wrong dude."

"I don't think so."

"If I can't persuade you to ditch him, what can I do you for?"

Jake answered, "We need a couple of guns."

"Thought that might be it." Kendall stepped aside so Jake

could join him behind the counter. They conferred for several minutes before Jake picked out two handguns, a small revolver for Rachel and a larger automatic for Jake.

Kendall brought out ammunition for each weapon, and the two men proceeded to give Rachel a short course in gun safety and operation. When they were finished, she put the revolver in her purse where it felt like a dead weight.

"Don't go shooting any cops," Kendall said.

"It's not for cops."

"If you say so."

Jake hesitated for a moment, then said, "If any of them come by asking questions, say you haven't seen us."

"You got it," Kendall answered, and he didn't ask why they needed the firepower.

When they were back in the car, Jake said, "I wish you could have some actual target practice. But we'd have to drive out of the city, then back again."

"I don't like carrying a gun at all. Let's hope I don't have to shoot."

"I feel better knowing we're not walking into an unknown situation unarmed."

A thought occurred to her, and she said, "Wait a minute. You didn't pay him."

"I don't have to."

"Because you're holding something over him?"

"No. I'm part owner of the shop."

She stared at him. "Part owner."

He shrugged. "I go to a lot of estate sales. There are always things I pick up that are worth buying but don't fit into my antiques business. So I asked Kendall if he wanted to go in on a pawnshop with me."

"Let me guess. You put up all of the money."

He kept his gaze steady. "Does that matter?"

"Just trying to get a handle on Jake Harper."

"It's a convenient arrangement for me. I can sell merchandise that wouldn't work for my upscale clientele."

"And it's convenient for him, too. I'll bet he lives in the building, right?"

"Yeah."

"But it's more than that for you. You like being his friend."

"What do you mean by that?"

"I mean, you use the friendship as a way to connect with… humanity."

He nodded.

"An adaptation mechanism."

"You mean like your connecting with humanity by reading tarot cards?"

"Yes. I guess we both found substitutes for real intimacy."

Jake reached for her hand, and they held on to each other, both thinking about how much their lives had changed.

For long moments neither of them spoke aloud until Jake said, "We should get some food. Better not to face the enemy on an empty stomach."

"Is he the enemy?"

"I guess we'll find out."

While they were still in the neighborhood, he stopped at a take-out luncheonette and got them each a poor boy and a soft drink.

Then they drove to the address he'd given the mystery caller. The two-story brick building looked as if it had formerly been a garage.

Jake stepped inside the door and keyed in a code on an alarm system pad, then he turned on a few lights.

As they walked into the huge room, Rachel saw it was being used as a storage facility for Mardi Gras floats. They were partially dismantled, but Rachel looked around in wonder at the displays. A sea monster was against one wall, next to a giant king and queen. Across from them was an artificial lawn with a tree in the middle. The branches were adorned with monkeys holding necklaces and other glittery treasure.

Behind the monkey tree was a set of giant musical instruments that looked as though they needed no human performers.

"I've seen some of these floats at the parade."

"They get refurbished and used from year to year."

"How do you have access to this place?"

"It belongs to the Buccaneer Crew," he said, naming one of the groups that sponsored Mardi Gras floats every year. "And I'm on the board of directors."

Another surprise.

I'm full of surprises, he silently answered.

"Are you going to lock the door?"

"No. We might as well make it easy for Mickey to come in. But we'll stay hidden until we get a good look at him."

As he spoke, he strode toward a set of metal stairs. She followed him to the top, where they stepped onto a balcony with a view of the floor below. Behind it was an office with windows looking out over the floats. Because they didn't turn the lights on in the office, the only illumination came from the ceiling fixtures above the warehouse floor.

Jake took something out of a desk drawer that he slipped into his pocket.

When they sat down at the desk to eat the meal they'd brought, Rachel shuddered.

This place gives me the creeps.

The place, or the situation?

Both. She stared at the sandwich she'd unwrapped. *I'm not real hungry.*

But we should eat. We'll be in better shape if we do.

They ate part of the sandwiches and wrapped up the rest.

"Is there another way out of here, besides down the stairs we came up?" she asked.

"The balcony turns a corner. You can't see from here, but there's another set of stairs that leads to a back door."

"Good. I'd hate to be trapped up here."

"I wouldn't have come up if that had been the case."

She glanced at her watch. "We still have almost three hours to wait. Maybe we should…practice."

He gave her a wolfish grin.

"I wasn't thinking of *that*."

It's how we forged the link. It's how we increased the connection.

She looked around and knew he picked up her distaste for the setting.

Okay. Not such a great place to make love. What did you have in mind? he asked.

Seeing how far away we can get from each other and still talk like this—without speaking aloud.

He looked from her to the balcony outside the office. *I don't like the idea of letting you out of my sight. Not when we don't know when that guy will show up.*

I think we've got plenty of time.

We don't know for sure.

While they were talking mind to mind, she stepped out the door and onto the balcony, closing the door behind her.

Come back! he shouted inside her head.

I can still hear you.

Through the window, he glared at her.

She walked farther along the balcony and stopped about twenty-five feet from where he stood.

Now? she asked.

Not as easy.

They could still see each other. She turned her back, facing out toward the warehouse floor, where she could look down on the giant floats. Then she backed up so that her shoulders were pressed against the wall.

How about now?

Not much. He was silent for several moments, then said inside her head, *Rub...your finger...across your lips.*

The communication was very faint, just a whisper in her mind, but she asked, *Why?*

See if the physical sensation makes it easier for me to reach your mind.

Is that all you can think about, physical sensation?

Just try it.

She lifted her hand and did as he'd asked. It could have been a neutral gesture, but she focused on the sensual component.

That's nice, Jake said, and his voice inside her head was stronger than it had been a moment ago. He must be right about the physical part.

You can feel me touching my lips? she asked.

Yes.

Then you do it, too.

She caught a flicker of male objection.

It's okay for me, but not for you?

He made a low sound that she heard in her mind before she felt him stroke his finger against his lips. He was right. It was nice.

Open your mouth. Stroke the inside of your lips, he told her.

By now she was liking the game, and in truth, it helped ease some of the tension of waiting for the unknown Mickey to show up.

She pressed her shoulders more firmly against the wall and parted her lips, then slipped her finger inside and played with the sensitive skin.

Nice. I'd like to feel you lick your finger with that cute little tongue of yours.

My tongue is cute?

To me.

Again she followed his direction, letting the sensuality of the moment wrap around her.

Take your other hand and cup your breast, then run your fingers over the nipple.

The request brought her up sharply. *No.*

Why not?

That's going too far.

You can hear me a lot better than you could a few minutes ago, can't you?

Yes.

I want to feel your response when you touch your breasts.

She wasn't willing to comply. Instead, she let herself focus on the physical sensations that came from him.

This is turning you on.

You know it is. You, too.

It's indecent, she protested.

Nothing we do together is indecent. Not if we both enjoy it.

She could have debated the point. Instead, she stood with her eyes closed, feeling the sense of connection with Jake.

Touch your breast.

This time she let herself go with the flow, raising her hand and stroking her finger across a hardened nipple.

Her own touch sent a jolt of sensation through her. Through him, too, because she knew he felt it.

We should stop this, she said.

Stay with me.

What are you going to do, have me start taking off my clothes out here on the balcony?

We both know that's not a good idea.

But this is? Instead of just playing, we should see if we can do something with our minds.

Like what?

I don't know. Make something on one of the floats move. Or turn the lights on and off without touching the switch.

You want to give up this game for something constructive?
She heard the grin in his voice.

Yes. Come out here.

You're getting ambitious. What float do you want to focus on?

I don't know. Help me choose.

He was walking to the office door when she heard a low buzzing sound. It didn't come from her ears. It was something Jake was hearing.

Chapter Ten

What was that?

That's the alarm I set when we came in. Someone's here. Stay against the wall and move back to the office.

Sudden dread coursed through her as she peered into the darkened warehouse. Mickey had arranged a meeting, but he was here way early. Like her and Jake he was being cautious, or maybe he'd come prepared to set something up.

She was almost to the door of the office when Jake stepped out, easing the door closed before walking quietly toward her. She inched toward him, and he reached for her hand and pressed his shoulder against hers. He was carrying her purse in his free hand, and he gave it to her.

She knew it was because that was where she'd put her gun.

When Jake gave her a meaningful look, she slung the strap of the purse across her chest, then opened it so she could see the revolver, feeling as if she'd stepped into a scene in a cop show.

The weapon should have made her feel safer. Instead, she felt a kind of raw exposure that she couldn't explain. It was kind of like when she and Jake had been playing around. They'd been focusing on physical sensations and sending silent messages. Somehow she felt as though the guy who'd come in was probing on the same wavelength.

He'd stayed out of sight. Now he walked to the middle

of the floor. He was medium height, with blond hair. From where they were standing, they couldn't see his eyes, but his posture was relaxed as he thrust his hands into the pockets of his jeans.

He looked around, then called, "Come out. I know you're up there."

"We'll stay here," Jake called back.

The guy shrugged.

"And you are…?" Jake asked.

"Mickey Delaney. And you are Jake Harper and Rachel Gregory."

"How do you know?"

"You got into some trouble when a woman named Evelyn Morgan was killed."

Jake remained silent, and Rachel took her cue from him.

"What did she tell you?" Mickey asked.

"Nothing. We didn't get a chance to talk to her."

"Who killed her?"

"I'd like to know. You said you had information for us. All you're doing is asking questions about Evelyn Morgan," Jake said. "What do you have to say that you couldn't say over the phone?"

"I think the two of you have recently discovered a talent that you didn't have before."

Jake didn't acknowledge the observation.

"Don't be modest about it. I'm sure you're enjoying it."

"What kind of talent?" Jake asked.

"Mind-to-mind communication."

Rachel caught her breath.

"How do you know?" Jake asked.

"Because I have it, too," the guy said.

"Where did it come from?"

Mickey shrugged. "I was hoping you had some insights."

"I was hoping you did," Jake countered.

"You got it when the two of you…hooked up," Mickey said.

"What about it?"

"What can you do?"

Don't even think about it, Jake said to Rachel.

"You first," Jake said.

"I thought you'd want to brag about your new abilities."

"This isn't getting us anywhere," Jake said. "Either tell us what you want or get the hell out of here."

"You're giving orders?"

It wasn't Mickey who spoke. A woman stepped from behind the float with the king and queen and looked up at them.

"This is my partner, Tanya," Mickey said.

She was a pretty, petite blonde with long wavy hair and a nicely proportioned figure, the kind of woman who would be attractive to a lot of men. But there was a hardness in her face that told him that anyone who got involved with her would be sorry. Like maybe Mickey.

She was dressed in jeans, a T-shirt and running shoes, but she was probably just as comfortable in high heels and a tight skirt.

"Did you come to give us lessons?" Jake asked with an edge to his voice.

"Not likely."

Tanya raised her hand and a bolt of lightning shot toward them, landing on the metal surface of the steps directly in front of their feet.

Jake and Rachel were already pressed against the wall of the office in back of them. The connection between them had been at its strongest. It weakened when they jumped apart.

Jake cursed, scrabbling for Rachel's mind, struggling to tell her what he wanted. But she was on his wavelength. She leaped back toward him and reached for his hand, grabbing on to him as he strove to find new resources inside himself. Imitating what the other couple had done, he sent a bolt of energy back toward the floor where the man and woman stood. It fell far short. And it was much less powerful than what the people below had conjured up.

Tanya laughed. "Is that the best you can do?"

"Why are you doing this?" Rachel shouted.

"Because we're the only ones who can have this power."

"How are we hurting you?" Rachel asked.

"By your existence."

As they talked, Jake tried to summon an attack with more power. Before he could do it, another bolt shot up at them. It hit Jake's leg, and he felt his muscles spasm, sending searing pain shooting through the limb.

Fighting the agony, he reached for the gun in his waist-band, but when his fingers closed around the metal, it turned scorching hot. He made a low sound as he dropped the weapon. It clattered to the balcony surface, then over the edge and onto the floor below.

Mickey ran to scoop it up, but Tanya restrained him with a hand on his shoulder.

The little scene below had given Jake and Rachel a few moments to get away.

Head for the back exit, Jake shouted inside her mind. *Go left.*

Rachel started running, but she stopped when she saw he could hardly walk on the wounded leg, much less run.

You're hurt.

Go on.

No.

She grabbed his hand, pulling him along. Another bolt hit him, and he doubled over, fighting unconsciousness. But he would not pass out. If he did, they were done for.

Fumbling in his pocket, he brought out the remote control

that he'd taken from the drawer, and began pushing buttons. Below them, the figures on some of the floats began to move. The king and queen raised and lowered their arms and turned their heads. The musical instruments began to play.

Mickey and Tanya whirled as the warehouse came to life around them.

"What the hell?"

"It's a trick. Focus on them," Tanya answered Mickey's exclamation.

She hadn't spoken aloud, but Jake caught the words that Tanya silently shouted.

She gave Jake an evil look and began blasting at the balcony again. A bolt hit Jake in the stomach, knocking the breath out of him, and he knew that he couldn't take much more.

"Help me get my shirt off."

Rachel didn't ask why as she helped him tear the buttons open and pull his arms from the sleeves.

When it was off, he scrabbled at his pocket and pulled out the box of matches that he'd also taken from the drawer.

I'll do it.

As another bolt hit him, his legs gave way and he almost dropped the box.

But she grabbed them from him and struck a match, which she touched to the shirt. When it flared up, she tossed it down onto the float with the tree. The artificial leaves went up like a torch, sending a cloud of smoke into the air.

Below them, Mickey cursed and began to cough.

Jake could hear Tanya coughing, too. He could no longer see them. And mercifully, the energy bolts had stopped flying up from the level below. But more floats had caught fire, and the smoke was rising, enveloping him and Rachel.

He knew he couldn't go on. The attack had done something to him that he didn't understand. But his body felt life-

less, and his brain was hardly any better. Still, when Rachel
pulled on his arm, dragging him along, he tried to help her
as best he could.

She reached the upper door. When she drew it open,
blessed fresh air poured in, clearing his head a little.

Jake, you've got to help me.

He knew that if he didn't get away, she wouldn't leave
him, so he made a superhuman effort, shoving himself out
the door. They were at the top of a long flight of steps, and
he almost tumbled down headfirst.

"Can you make it down?"

"We'll see." Sending his thoughts to her had become impossible.

Gritting his teeth, he leaned on her like a drunken man as
she guided him down the steps to the alley and back to the
car.

"Keys?"

"Pocket."

She leaned him against the side of the vehicle while she
fumbled in his pocket, then pulled out the keys and shoved
the right one into the lock.

When she opened the back door, he slid inside and flopped
onto the seat.

He tried to hang on to consciousness, but it was too much
effort. All he wanted to do was sleep. Maybe forever.

RACHEL STARTED THE ENGINE and drove away from the warehouse. Smoke was now billowing from the roof.

Had Mickey and Tanya gotten away, or were they still in
there?

She gritted her teeth. Did it matter? They'd lured her and
Jake to the warehouse to kill them, and they'd almost succeeded.

Her heart pounded as she looked back at Jake. He was deep into unconsciousness, his mind completely shut off from her.

Still, she tried to reach him.

"Jake?"

Jake?

She kept repeating his name, trying to break through whatever barrier now separated them, but there was absolutely no response, and the lack of connection was like a punch in the gut. She'd come to depend on it, and now she didn't know what to do without it.

But she did know she had to get Jake somewhere safe. And she couldn't drive him far. She had to find out what was wrong with him.

A siren sounded in the distance, and she stiffened. But it wasn't a police car chasing her. It must be fire engines racing toward the Buccaneer Crew's burning warehouse.

Although she hated thinking of all those floats going up in smoke, burning them had been the only way for her and Jake to get away.

She kept driving, wondering where she was going, until she found herself in the alley in back of Kendall Wexler's pawnshop.

She sat with her head against the wheel, her arms embracing it for a moment. Then she got out and turned the knob on the back door of the building. It was open, and she rushed inside, making for the shop in the front.

When she charged into the room, Kendall Wexler was facing her. He'd been charming when she'd met him a few hours earlier. Now he stood with a gun in his hand, pointed at her middle. His eyes were hard as glass.

"What are you trying to pull?" he asked.

Her mouth had turned dry, and she had to moisten her lips before she could talk. "Jake's been hurt. I didn't know where else to take him."

"Shot?"

"No. He…"

"What happened to him?"

She didn't know how to describe what had happened. Not without a long explanation that Kendall probably wouldn't believe anyway. "Electricity," she said. "He's unconscious. In the car. Is there somewhere here where I can take care of him?"

The old man gave her a hard stare. "You're asking me to hide two people who are wanted for murder. That makes me an accessory after the fact."

"You know we didn't do it."

"I don't know a damn thing."

"You gave us guns."

"I gave them to Jake."

Her shoulders sagged. "Okay. I'll figure something out."

When she turned toward the door, he allowed her to leave.

She walked to the car, wondering where the hell she was going now. Probably a motel.

Opening the back door, she knelt beside Jake. His face was pale, and his breath was shallow.

Movement behind her made her stiffen.

It was Kendall. "There's a room where you can stay," he said in a gruff voice.

She wanted to refuse, but standing on principle wasn't going to help Jake.

"Thank you," she answered.

She climbed into the car and lifted Jake's shoulders. Kendall grabbed his legs, and together they got him out of the vehicle. Supporting him between them, they made their way slowly back to the shop.

Inside, the old man stopped halfway down the hall and opened a door to a small room with a twin bed covered by a threadbare chenille spread. With only a dresser, sink and faded armchair, the room wasn't plush, but it was a place to hide out.

"Guest room. You can stay here. There's a bathroom across the hall," he said, gesturing in its direction. "I'm going to close the shop and leave. Don't want to be involved in this."

"I understand," she said as they got Jake onto the bed. She covered his bare chest with the quilt folded at the end of the bed.

Kendall had backed toward the doorway. "You should hide the car."

"Where?"

"I got a garage a few doors down. I'll take the car there."

"Thank you," she said again.

"Mr. Jake done a lot for me."

"Yes."

When he closed the door, she turned back to Jake, unsure of what to do. How could she get him medical attention when they were wanted for murder? And would a doctor even know what to do for him? She'd be in the same fix she was in with Kendall, having to explain that he'd been in a psychic battle and gotten hit by mental thunderbolts.

Pulling down the quilt, she examined Jake's chest. As far as she could see, there was nothing wrong there.

But they'd hit him in the leg, she remembered. At least their aim hadn't been perfect. Thank God for small favors.

He didn't move when she unbuckled his belt, worked the button at the top of his jeans and lowered his zipper. Then she slipped off his shoes and set them on the floor. Trying not to move him around too much, she pulled his jeans down, then off.

The skin of his right leg was red and puckered, as if he'd been burned. She saw another burn on his belly. But not third-degree, thank God. His flesh wasn't charred. It looked more like a bad sunburn.

A tap at the door made her jump. When she opened it, Kendall handed her the keys. He looked beyond her to Jake, saw the wounds and shook his head.

"I'm leaving now," he said. "The car's two doors down—to the right."

"Thank you."

As he withdrew, her chest tightened. She wasn't sure if she could trust him, but Jake had, and she would rely on that, in the absence of other information.

She laid her hand on Jake's chest, reassured by the steady beating of his heart. Wondering what to do, she slipped off her own shoes and climbed onto the bed, putting her arms around him and holding him.

"We're at Kendall's place," she said. "We're safe. But I don't know what to do for you."

When he didn't answer, she closed her eyes, trying to reach him with her mind.

Jake, we're safe at Kendall's. He's letting us stay here, but he's nervous about it. Please wake up and tell me what to do.

When he still didn't respond, she repeated the message, hoping she was getting through to him, but she felt as if she was sending her thoughts into empty air.

The sensation terrified her. All her life, she'd been alone in a way that most people couldn't even imagine. Then she'd found Jake, and everything had changed.

And now...?

She knit her fingers with his, willing him to come back to her, but he only lay on the bed, his breath shallow. She knew that he was injured in some way she couldn't understand. It wasn't just because his leg was burned. They had done something that shut him off from the world—from her. He'd gotten out of the warehouse, but now he didn't seem to be aware of his surroundings at all.

And something else alarmed her, too.

His skin had begun to cool.

"Jake?"

He didn't move. Didn't give any indication that he knew she was there.

"Jake?" She heard the panic in her own voice, knew that she was on the verge of losing it. Losing him.

And if that happened, what would become of her? The old Rachel had told herself she was content with her life. That was before she'd found out there was something more. Something the two of them had that she'd never in her life imagined.

At this moment, it was gone. Vanished as though it had never existed. She was alone again.

She was sure she couldn't go on without him. Not when she knew how it had been between them.

Desperation welled inside her. She looked toward the door, then got up quickly and turned the lock, hoping that Kendall really was gone and that no one else would come in. Not now.

Standing beside the bed, she undressed, leaving only her panties.

When she'd climbed onto the bed again, she slid on top of Jake, pressing herself against him, trying to warm him with her body as she tried desperately to reach him with her mind.

With her cheek against his, she whispered his name, begging him to open himself to her. She used her voice and also a silent plea.

For long moments, nothing happened.

Then she felt a glimmer of recognition, but very weak.

"Jake?"

From far away, she heard the inner voice that had become so familiar to her.

Goodbye.

"No," she screamed in anguish. "No."

But he didn't answer.

Chapter Eleven

"No!" Rachel shouted again, aloud and in her mind. "No!"

But she knew he was gone—departed to a place where she couldn't follow.

With that terrible knowledge, she felt her own heart fracture, her own spirit die.

She was still screaming, still enveloped by the terrible agony of losing him. It was the worst pain she had ever felt. But out of the unimaginable grief came a new kind of resolve. She *would not* let it happen. Not now. Not when she had finally filled the terrible void in her life.

She must bring him back or die trying.

Determined to shut out the world, she squeezed her eyes tight and clung to him with her arms, her hands, her legs and her spirit. His soul was drifting upward, and she went with him.

No longer able to feel her own body, she stayed with Jake.

He hadn't answered her cries when he lay on the bed, but now he did. At least she had that much.

Go back, he shouted in her head.

Not without you.

I can't.

Are you a coward?

How can you ask that?

You're leaving but we have work to do.

They...killed me.

Don't let them win. If you let them win, we're both dead.

A long, empty silence followed. It might have lasted for seconds or minutes or hours.

She didn't know precisely where she and Jake were. They must be suspended somewhere between life and death. It could still go either way, she knew. But if she could pull him back to the world she would.

She clung to him with everything she had, trying to bring them both back to earth.

By tiny degrees, she felt something change. The balance was shifting. At first she couldn't be sure it was working. Then her heart leaped as she felt herself coming closer to the earth, bringing him with her. Against all odds, he was coming back, too.

Gradually she felt her own body, felt her arms wrapped around Jake, felt her breasts pressed to his chest.

And then the biggest miracle of all. She felt his arms come up and clasp her. Not tightly, but it was enough.

She opened her eyes. Through a film of tears, she found herself staring down into his face.

"Rachel?"

"Thank God."

"I was...dead. I should be...gone."

"I couldn't let it happen."

You brought me back.

Thank the Lord.

As she clung to him, more tears welled in her eyes, and she struggled to hold them back.

She had won. They had won.

When he rolled to his side, cradling her against him, she lost the battle and began to cry, the sobs racking her body.

His hand stroked over her back, tangled in her hair, giving her comfort.

Finally, she was able to get herself under control.

I thought I'd lost you.

You brought me back, he said again, awe and admiration in his voice.

What happened? What did they do to you?

Hit me with those energy bolts. I don't know what they did, exactly. Weakened me. I felt myself fading away.

You're still weak, I think.

He raised his head and looked around. "We're at Kendall's?" he said aloud, and she knew that the mental communication was draining him.

"His guest room."

"I've stayed here once or twice."

"Hiding out?"

"Yeah."

"From whom?"

"Those business associates I told you about."

"I thought he was going to shoot me when I first came in. He didn't want us staying here."

"He's got to be cautious."

He skimmed his lips over her cheek. "You were very brave."

"I just did…what I had to."

"More than you had to."

She didn't try to explain her overwhelming panic; she simply snuggled in his arms as they talked.

"Mickey and…the woman…"

"They're like us. I mean, they bonded—mentally."

"But they can't stand the idea of sharing their power with anyone else," he muttered.

"It's not sharing! We have nothing to do with them."

"Maybe they can't think in those terms."

"Why?"

"I think it's coming from Tanya. I caught the edge of her

thoughts. She's needy." He cleared his throat. "But it's more than that. I think she may be a psychopath."

"And she controls Mickey?"

"Apparently."

"Both of us were needy."

"Not like her."

"Thank God." She dragged in a breath and let it out. "They didn't even try to be friendly. They just attacked."

"They're a lot stronger than we are. We were lucky to get away."

"Did they?"

"I don't know. I was pretty out of it by the end."

"There was a lot of smoke," she murmured. "I couldn't see them.

"If they escaped, can they find us?" she asked in a voice she couldn't hold steady as she remembered the attack.

"I don't know," he answered, his voice weaker, and she knew he didn't even have the strength for this conversation.

She wanted to drag him out of bed, out of the city. Away to some safe place.

"They knew we were in New Orleans," she whispered.

"But they had to tell Patrick to call me," he whispered.

That calmed her a little. They were safe here. At least for now. "You need to sleep."

"Yeah." When he closed his eyes, she felt her chest tighten. But she reached out with her mind, feeling him with her. It was all right. He was just going to sleep. It wasn't like when he had slipped into unconsciousness.

"Let me cover you."

Mmm.

He raised his legs, and she pulled the quilt free before spreading it over him and settling down beside him.

She was exhausted, too, and she was asleep almost as soon as she closed her eyes.

For a long time, she was at peace. Then she slipped into a dream that she and Jake were far away, on a tropical island, lying in the warm sun. He leaned over to kiss her, and she smiled in her sleep.

When she felt his hand on her breast, she knew that the dream was part of their reality.

You're awake.

How are you? she asked.

He slid his hands around her bottom and pulled her against the erection straining at the front of his pants.

Fully recovered.

You need to rest.

I need you.

She might have argued, but she needed him, too. Needed to reaffirm everything that they had built between them.

When his tongue played with the seam of her lips, asking her to open for him, she did, closing her eyes as he explored the line of her teeth and stroked the sensitive tissue on the inside of her lips.

She heard herself make a small sound deep in her throat, telling him she liked what he was doing. But he knew that already, knew it from her mind.

She was open to him in a way that thrilled her. When his tongue dipped farther into her mouth, she felt hot, needy sensations curling through her body. And through his.

She sighed as his hands stroked over her hips, then upward to find the sides of her breasts, making her nipples tighten.

She needed more. So much more. But she knew from his mind that he wasn't going to rush this.

You brought me back.

I had to.

We need to celebrate. She heard the grin in his voice, and more. His silent words were like a solemn commitment.

An affirmation of what they had found together, and almost lost.

She reached up to run her fingers through his thick, dark hair. Then she slid one hand down his back, slipping it under the waistband of his shorts.

They're in the way.

So are your panties.

She saw him grinning as they both rolled away so they could kick off their underwear, then come gratefully back into each other's arms. The lengths of their bodies pressed together.

Sensations bombarded her. What she was feeling. What he felt.

"Yes," he murmured, his mouth still on her.

She was dizzy with desire for him.

When he gathered her closer, words of gratitude rose in his throat.

It was difficult to draw in a full breath, difficult to think.

She made a small sobbing sound as he rolled her to her back, playing his hands over her throbbing nipples before taking one hard peak into his mouth, drawing on her as he used his thumb and finger on the other side.

Please, now.

Soon.

He slid one hand down her body, into her hot, moist folds as he lifted his head to look down at her.

She saw passion mold his features, felt her hips lift restlessly against his fingers.

Her eyes met his, and everything inside her clenched.

When his body sank into hers, she cried out at the joining.

She was so overcome with emotion she couldn't speak as he began to move inside her. But they didn't need words.

She threw her head back onto the pillow while she matched

his rhythm. Her fingers dug into his shoulders as they both climbed toward orgasm.

She felt him holding back, felt him waiting for her to reach the peak of her pleasure. But she moved her hips in a frantic rhythm, pushing them both toward climax. Finally it rocketed through her, and through him, and they clung together, feeling the universe tilt and sway around them.

They came back to earth gently, still clinging together.

Oh, Jake.

I love you.

She had longed to hear those words from him. Now she wondered…

Not because you brought me back. I knew how I felt. I couldn't say it. I didn't dare think it.

The words trembled at the edge of her mind. She clung to him as he rolled to his side and settled her against him.

I knew it, too. Even when I never expected it in my life.

But it's not enough, he finished the thought. *Not yet.*

I need to feel safe.

I know. We will.

When?

She knew he couldn't answer, and she also knew that their time together might be limited.

No! he protested.

We still don't know about the clinic. The man who killed Evelyn Morgan is still chasing us. The police still think we're involved. We've assaulted a detective. And now another man and woman have shown up and tried to wipe us from the face of the earth. They almost killed you.

It sounds bad, but we'll figure it out.

She desperately wanted to believe him, but too much had happened too fast.

We're strong together, his thoughts told her.

Strong enough?

Yes.

She knew he would have given her that answer, no matter what he really thought.

We will be strong enough. You were right. We have to practice.

Yes.

"I'm going out to get us something to eat."

Her hand tightened on his arm. "Too dangerous. I'll do it."

"No. This is no neighborhood for a woman to be walking around at night."

She sighed. "Okay."

When he climbed out of bed, she looked at his leg and his stomach.

He followed her gaze.

"How do those…burns feel?"

"Not great. But I'll live." His gaze bore into her. "Thanks to you."

She could only nod as she watched him dress.

"You still have the gun we got here earlier?"

"Yes."

That made her remember what had happened at the warehouse.

"You threw down the gun you had."

"Yeah. It turned burning hot."

He zipped his jeans and told her, "Lock the door and keep the weapon with you until I come back."

As soon as he had left, she got out of bed and pulled her clothes on. Then she took the revolver out of her purse and made a quick trip across the hall to the bathroom before returning and locking the door.

As she sat on the bed, she sent her mind toward Jake, trying to contact him. She couldn't reach him, but it wasn't like when he'd been leaving his body. She knew he was still on earth, and that knowledge was reassuring.

Then she sensed the edge of his thoughts and focused in on them. Her heart beat faster as she felt him coming toward her.

Finally he spoke.

Unlock the door.

She got up and let him in. As soon as he'd set bags and a pasteboard tray with cups down on the table, she hugged him.

"I didn't like letting you out of my sight. Or out of my *hearing*."

"Me neither."

They pulled out seats at the table. He'd brought poor boys and cups of strong New Orleans coffee. With cream and sugar for her.

Did you find out about the warehouse?

He answered as he took a bite of the sandwich. *The fire department saved the building, but the floats are destroyed.*

Sorry!

I'll pay for them.

She started to say it wasn't his fault, but he shook his head. *I burned the place up.*

To save our lives.

They ate in silence for a few minutes before she said, *So how did Mickey and his girlfriend find us?*

He took a sip of coffee as he said, *Convenient that you can talk and eat at the same time.*

When she laughed, he went on. *The Evelyn Morgan murder made the news. That would be a clue. Maybe they headed down here and then got more...um...vibes when they got to the city. Who knows what they can do.*

She nodded. "And who knows what *we* can do, if we keep working at it. They may have done us a favor—showing us real power."

He grinned, then sobered. *We have to assume Evelyn Morgan knew about the clinic.*

Or suspected. And thought it had affected us. Maybe she didn't know how. And what about Eric Smithson, the guy who killed her, then tried to tie me up in my shop?

I'm assuming that he doesn't know. And he's trying to find out.

She thought about that as she ate. *Why does he care?*

I assume it's not because he's worried about liability from the old experiments.

He could be like Mickey and Minnie.

Minnie! I'm sure she'd hate being called that. But back to Smithson. I don't think he's got any psychic abilities. He's using conventional methods. And he was shocked by the window image I put into his head.

Right.

And we can't go to the cops about him. Or about Mickey and Minnie.

When they'd finished the meal, Jake said, "We should get out of here."

"Where are we going this time?"

"First, to practice our thunderbolt skills."

"You mean like what the Odd Couple did to you."

"Odd Couple! Like us."

"But we're not as odd yet," she pointed out.

"Yeah. I shot a bolt back at them, but it hardly had any power. I didn't even know we could do that."

"How do we get more power?"

"Like I said, practice."

"On what?"

"We can go out into the swamp and try to zap some trees." He started for the door, then stopped. "Where's the car?"

"Kendall said it was in a garage a few doors down."

When Rachel started to straighten up the bed, Jake helped her. Together they folded the quilt and stuffed the trash into the bag from the fast-food restaurant.

Jake turned to inspect the room. "It looks like nobody was even here."

"Maybe we should wipe away our fingerprints. And take the sheets."

"Yeah. Not a bad idea."

They used paper towels from the bathroom to wipe all the hard surfaces they might have touched and bundled up the bedding before leaving.

The car was where Kendall had left it.

When they had pulled into the alley, Jake asked, "You have some idea where to find the clinic?"

"South…and west."

"How do you know?"

She reached into her purse and closed her fingers around the deck of tarot cards, letting impressions come to her the way they did during a reading. "I have a feeling we'll be headed in the right direction. And when we get closer, I may have a better idea."

You're the psychic.

You seem to have developed some talents we can use.

As they drove out of town, Rachel said, "We were pretty busy when we had our meeting with Mickey and Minnie, but we should see what we can figure out about them."

"Like what?"

"Well, they looked like they were about our age."

"Right. And they both had Southern accents, but not too pronounced. Maybe they were born around here and moved away."

She thought for a moment. "They found each other a while ago and worked on their talent—unless they just plain have more ability than we do."

"I think it's the former."

"We hope."

Jake swung his gaze toward her, then back to the road. "You think we're going to meet them again?"

She felt a shiver go over her skin. "I wish it weren't true, but I do think we will."

"You think they got out of the warehouse?"

"Yes."

"Well, that's one advantage we've got over them—you. I doubt that either of them is a tarot card reader."

She murmured her assent. When she'd gotten interested in the field, she hadn't thought that it might save her own life.

Jake squeezed her hand, and she knew he'd picked up the thought.

"Anything else we know about them?" he asked.

"They've been practicing for a while."

The conversation petered out, and they sat in silence until Jake pointed to a secondary road.

"How about we go there for target practice?"

"As good a place as any."

They turned off the highway onto a narrow road barely wide enough for two cars to pass. But there was no traffic coming toward them.

The road soon went from blacktop to gravel. Trees thick with Spanish moss crowded in on either side. She looked out the window trying to spot any houses that might be in the area, but she saw only swamp vegetation and pools of water covered with duckweed. An alligator plopped into the water as they passed.

Jake found a patch of relatively dry ground, and they both got out, crunching over gravel, then stopping to stare around them at the peaceful scene. It was damp and dark under the trees and probably ten degrees cooler than in the city.

"If we attack the trees, we're going to scare the birds," Rachel said, looking over at some egrets wading in the shallow water of a bayou and standing on the far shore.

"Let's hope we can."

"What did you do when you sent that mental thunderbolt toward Mickey and Minnie?"

"I'm not sure. We were under attack. After I saw them do it, I just thought of calling up energy, then sending it in a stream toward them."

"Okay. Let's try it."

They walked a little way from the car and stood shoulder to shoulder, their hands clasped.

You direct it, Rachel said, since she had no idea what he had done at the warehouse.

He pointed toward a tree about twenty feet away. *I'll see if I can hit the trunk.*

She watched Jake focus on the trunk, felt his body tense as he gathered his concentration. She wasn't sure what he was doing, but she knew he was trying to re-create his actions in the battle. Her heart started to pound as he stood for long seconds with his fingers clamping hers in a death grip. When nothing happened, he made a disgusted sound.

"Maybe they blasted it out of me." The observation was followed by a curse. "Nothing's there. If they come back and attack us, what are we going to do, crawl under the table?"

Chapter Twelve

Carter Frederick, alias Eric Smithson, felt his stomach tie itself in knots. He didn't want to make the call, but it was his only alternative.

When the Badger picked up the phone, Carter dragged in a breath and let it out.

"I need some help from you," he said.

"Were you involved in a New Orleans warehouse fire?" the man on the other end of the line said.

"No."

"And you don't have Gregory and Harper?"

"No. There's something about them. Something they're using to get away. Maybe you'd better tell me what it is." He'd never demanded anything from the Badger, and he held his breath now, waiting for an answer.

"If I knew, I'd tell you."

"Where would they go?" he pressed. "Where should I look for them?"

"Houma, Louisiana," the Badger answered.

"Why?"

"They may be trying to get information about the Solomon Clinic."

"Why?"

This time the line went dead.

RACHEL SQUEEZED JAKE'S hand. *It's not gone. There's no reason it would be.*

How about the fact that they almost killed me?

But you're here. We're...communicating mind to mind. That's not gone.

Then why isn't the firepower working? She heard the anger and anxiety in his voice.

Determined to stay calm, despite the beating of her heart, she said, *Let's think about it. What did you do when you were fighting them?*

He flapped his arm. *I don't know. I just did it.*

They stood in silence for several moments, and she knew he was on the verge of turning and stomping back to the car.

She wondered if he would let her help, but she didn't have to ask.

She felt his resistance. He wasn't used to someone else taking over for him. Specifically, he wasn't used to *her* doing it, but after a long moment, he gave a mental shrug.

For a split second she thought about giving up before she started. At least he'd be able to say she'd failed, too.

I'm not that stupid.

Sorry. Just a passing impulse.

Clasping his hand more tightly, she ordered herself to relax. When she'd taken several deep breaths, she reached within herself, striving for the kind of state when she was reading the cards for a customer and trying to get more information than was just in the deck. Only, now she was grasping for potent energy, not insights into someone's life. And she wasn't quite sure how to do it.

Maybe this will help.

As he'd done when she'd been reading the cards that Evelyn Morgan had handled, Jake shifted his position so that he was standing behind her, his front pressed to her back. He stroked his hands up and down her arms, then leaned forward to slide his lips against her cheek.

She closed her eyes as he shifted his mouth so that he could use his teeth on her ear. Arousal began to build inside her, and she might have told him that was a distraction, but it wouldn't have been the truth.

He moved his hands inward, cupping her breasts, pressing and kneading, making her nipples harden.

She could feel him smiling as he stroked his thumbs back and forth across the sensitized peaks, taking her arousal up another notch.

A thought flashed in her mind. His thought. Of turning her around and pressing her against the nearest tree trunk.

But she knew he wasn't going to do it, not when he could tell that the heat building between them was generating the power that she was trying to find.

It simmered inside her, and she let it grow, feeling energy coursing through her into Jake and back again so that they were acting in concert, only he was letting her direct the process.

When the energy had built to some kind of tipping point, she held out her hand, toward a tree about sixty feet away. A flash of light sprang from her fingers, and she saw the bolt strike, watched it splinter and pop.

Jake silently approved. *You've got the talent.*

You know it wasn't just me. I couldn't do it without the energy you added.

But you knew how to do it.

Not exactly. I tried what I've learned from years of practice of reading people.

It's the same?

Not exactly, but something similar.

She felt his annoyance that he couldn't do it.

You did it when we needed to fight them, her thoughts told him.

Not well enough.

That's why we're here—to get better at it.

She felt his acknowledgment, but she understood that he wanted to be the one to direct the attack. He was the guy. He should be the warrior.

Let's try again, he told her.

Sure.

This time when she let the power grow inside her, she tried to make him part of what was happening.

I feel it!

She built the energy but mentally stepped back and let him direct a bolt toward another tree.

When the blast crashed against the trunk, she felt his satisfaction.

Thanks.

You did it.

You let me take charge.

And you could.

He turned her in his arms, bringing his mouth down to hers for a hard, thankful kiss.

For long moments they feasted on each other, exchanging thoughts and so much more.

It was dumb of me to insist on being the one in control.

Of course not.

Pull me back when I'm being stubborn.

Only if you do the same for me.

Finally he lifted his head.

Back to work.

If you say so, boss.

He laughed. *Only when you want me to be.*

They stayed in the swampy area for another forty minutes,

repeating the process, elation building inside them as they became better at controlling the mental weapon.

Let's try it without touching.

They dropped hands and moved a few feet apart. It was harder to summon up the energy blast, and it was less effective, but they could still do it—until they were about ten feet apart.

When both of them began to waver on their feet, he squeezed her hand.

"Enough."

"Probably not. If we can't do it perfectly, we're in danger."

"But if we keep it up, we won't be able to walk back to the car."

When they returned to the vehicle, he leaned his head back and closed his eyes.

"I'm so hungry I could eat an alligator."

She laughed. "There's probably a restaurant around here where you can get it. Out here in the country, I've had it fried like chicken fingers and served with hot sauce."

"Let's go for it."

He backed the car around, and they pulled out of the swampy area and back onto the main road.

They found a small restaurant in the next town they came to, and it did have alligator bites on the menu.

"It might as well be chicken," Jake observed as he ate them.

"Anything weird tastes like chicken."

When they were back in the car again, he said, "I want to try something else."

"I sensed that."

"But you didn't know what I was thinking?"

She shook her head.

"Good. I was working hard to keep it from you."

"Because it's something bad?"

"No. Because that's another skill we should try to develop."

"I guess that's right." She waited a moment before saying, "I get the feeling we're not going back to the swamp."

He found a small motel, where they checked in. When they'd brought their luggage inside and locked the door, she looked at him.

You want to try to figure out where to find that clinic.

Yes.

As he spoke inside his head, he reached for her, pulling her into his arms.

She let herself sink against him, simply absorbing the fact of being together. Every moment with him was precious because she knew how quickly it could all be snatched away from them.

We're going to win.

She didn't answer. Everything would either work out for them…or it wouldn't.

Since when did you get so fatalistic?

Since people started coming at me with guns and thunderbolts.

We'll beat them all.

She liked his confidence and knew she was in the hands of the man who had pulled himself up from nothing to become a prominent New Orleans businessman. He'd done it when the odds were against him, which made him a good man to have on her side. Still, she couldn't let herself bet on them without more evidence.

Then we'd better get to work.

He gathered her to him, lowering his mouth to hers for a kiss that instantly started the blood running hotly in her veins. He'd kissed her like that out in the swamp. Now they were in a nice private motel room, where they could do anything they wanted.

Don't get too comfortable, he warned, opening himself fully to her.

She made a strangled sound when she realized what he had in mind.

You devil!

Do you have a better idea?

Since she didn't have a good answer, she let him continue down the path he'd started on.

When he reached under her shirt and unhooked her bra, she leaned away from him so that he could pull the garment up and cup her breasts, gliding his thumbs over the crests, which instantly hardened at his touch.

He unbuttoned her shirt, then slipped it off along with her bra and tossed it onto the chair.

When she was naked to the waist, he unbuttoned his shirt and shrugged it off before pulling her back into his arms, swaying her upper body against his, making her cry out at the erotic sensations.

When she thought she'd fall over he lowered her to the bed.

Safer that way, he murmured in her mind as his hands stroked over her back while he nibbled at her ear with his teeth.

She closed her eyes and stroked his broad shoulders, trying to get as close to him as she could. Not just physically but mentally, as well.

She was on fire for him, but they'd made a silent agreement not to satisfy their cravings for each other. At least not until they'd accomplished their goal. Which was why they were still half-dressed as they rocked together on the bed.

Take us back to the clinic, he finally said, his silent voice urgent inside her head.

Arousal brought their minds together in a way that would have been impossible a few days ago.

At that moment in time, they were truly one as she sent her thoughts spinning back to the clinic where her mom had taken her years before.

Once again she saw the children playing with the toys scattered about the floor. And the parents in the seats around the room, watching.

Last time, she and Jake had sent only their minds here. This time was different.

She and Jake were actually standing at the side of the room, like two ghosts invisible to everyone around them.

Everyone?

She struggled not to gasp as a little girl looked up at her and Jake. As their eyes met across the space of eight feet—and twenty-five years—she went rigid.

The child looking at them was the little girl Rachel. She tipped her head to the side, studying them with a bright curiosity that made Rachel's chest tighten. Confronting her earlier self like this was the strangest thing she had ever done.

Quickly, she looked down, relieved that in this scene, the shirt she'd been wearing earlier was back on her body.

Relief gave way to panic when she tried to speak into Jake's mind, but found she couldn't do it.

"Yeah, strange," Jake murmured. "In a lot of ways."

"You can't talk in my mind, either?"

"No."

When the girl spoke, Rachel's focus shifted back to her. "I never saw you here before. Who are you?" she asked.

"Visitors," the adult Rachel answered.

The girl looked back at her mother, who was talking to one of the other women.

"Do I know you?" the young Rachel asked.

"You will when you grow up."

"And then I won't be alone?"

Rachel's heart squeezed at the question and the wistful

quality of her child voice. Even back then, she'd known that feeling of separation from the rest of humanity.

"It's going to turn out okay," she whispered, hoping she was telling the truth. Well, at least the part about Jake was true. If they could just find a way to defeat all the forces bent on destroying them.

In the vision, Jake pressed his shoulder to hers, and she leaned against him, grateful that he was here with her and she didn't have to face this strange situation alone.

"You'll find someone really special," she whispered to her younger self.

The girl's gaze flicked to Jake. "Like you have?"

"Yes."

The young Rachel nodded solemnly.

As if aware of something out of the ordinary going on, Mrs. Gregory looked over at her little daughter, and Rachel pressed her lips together.

"Is something wrong, dear?" her mother asked in an anxious voice.

"No," the child answered quickly. She gave the adult Rachel one more look before turning back to the toy farm on the floor in front of her. She was playing with an intensity that told Rachel she was still interested in the visitors, but she didn't want her mother to ask her any more questions.

Jake reached for Rachel's hand, and together they edged around the room, heading for the door. But the closer they got, the harder it was to make any progress. It was as if they were underwater, pushing against a strong current that had flowed there to keep them back.

"It's resisting us," Jake muttered.

Rachel tried to answer silently, but that was still impossible.

"Why?" she whispered.

He shrugged, then spoke in a low voice. "We shouldn't be

here in the first place. Maybe you've already broken one law of the universe by talking to yourself."

"What law?"

He shrugged again. "I don't know any more about this than you do." He turned his head toward her. "Didn't you ever read any time-travel stories?"

"Not my thing. I wasn't into science fiction."

"Just the paranormal."

"I guess."

"Do you remember the conversation with the visitor—from when you were little?"

She swallowed. "I didn't. But I think I do now."

"Oh?"

"We shouldn't keep talking. I mean, we might draw more attention to ourselves."

"Right," he answered in a whisper as he tightened his grip on her hand and kept moving toward the door, ushering her along.

She let him lead. Maybe because he was bigger and stronger, he made better progress against the thickened air that formed an invisible wall in front of them.

They were almost to the door, when a loud voice rang out. "What's going on here?"

Chapter Thirteen

Jake swung around to see who had spoken. It was a young, nicely dressed woman with dark hair, light-colored eyes and a questioning expression on her face. He had the feeling he'd seen her before. It took a moment to place her, but when he realized who she was, his heart skipped a beat. It was Evelyn Morgan.

Rachel had also turned and was staring at the woman.

"What are you doing here?" Evelyn asked in a brisk voice.

"Sorry. I…uh…I think we're at the wrong place," he managed to say, although his mouth was suddenly so dry that he could hardly speak.

Her eyes narrowed as she looked at them. "You shouldn't be in here unless you have business with Dr. Solomon."

They must have become more solid and real looking while they'd been in the clinic. Or maybe Evelyn had the same ability as the young Rachel. In her case, because she'd seen them before, and she recognized them.

No, wait. Not before. Later.

Trying to figure that out had his head swimming. Still, he knew what they had to do.

"I'm sorry. We're leaving," he said quickly, hoping they could get out the door before Evelyn came over.

"Just a minute."

Ignoring her, he kept walking with Rachel at his side.

It had been hard to walk toward the door, but it seemed that Evelyn Morgan's voice had broken the spell that kept them in the room.

He reached the exit, turned the door handle and walked out into bright sunshine.

Rachel let out the breath she must have been holding.

"It was her," she said. "She was younger, but it was her."

"Yes. When she took a step, I saw the limp."

"Did she work there?"

"I don't know. Maybe she had some other business at the place."

She turned to look at the plate beside the door. Now she could read it, and it said Solomon Clinic.

The door behind them opened, and Evelyn Morgan stepped out.

"I want to talk to you."

"I'm afraid not." Jake tightened his grip on Rachel's hand and started down the street.

He was worried that Evelyn Morgan would follow, but he heard no footsteps behind him.

In the distance he heard a police siren.

"Are they coming for us because we weren't authorized to be in there?"

"I don't know."

"Now what?"

He knew how they had traveled to the past. He hoped to hell they could leave using the same technique, but not in front of anyone else.

His heart was pounding as he ducked between a hardware store and a restaurant called the Waterside, coming to an abrupt stop when he found they were facing a bayou. The restaurant had a wooden deck overlooking the water, with tables where patrons could eat.

He and Rachel climbed onto the deck, out of the passage-way between the buildings.

"Now what?" Rachel gasped as she looked around. "She must have seen where we went."

The deck projected over the water, where he could see a turtle swimming and an alligator on the opposite bank.

Rachel followed his gaze. "We're trapped."

"No. We don't have to stay here."

Jake turned her toward him, wrapping his arms around her as he pulled her close.

"Think only of me," he murmured as he brought his mouth down on hers.

He tried to ignore the sound of voices coming toward them and closed his eyes, focusing intently on the woman in his arms. The feel of her body pressed to the length of his. The urgency of her kiss. The sensation of his hands traveling up and down her body, molding her hips to his.

The world seemed to swirl around them, and he fought a dizzying sensation. It felt as though the two of them were caught in a whirlwind, being lifted off their feet and thrown through the air.

Rachel gasped and clung to him, and all he could do was wrap her more tightly in his embrace.

He tried to thrust away the idea that they were going to get caught. And then what? Would they be stuck here? Well, that was one solution to their problems. If they stayed back here in time, the cops in New Orleans wouldn't be after them. Maybe they could even save Evelyn Morgan's life.

As those thoughts chased themselves through his brain, he found that he and Rachel weren't standing anymore. They were lying on a bed.

He opened his eyes and looked around, trying to remember where he was—and when.

The scene solidified, and he knew they were back in the motel room.

He couldn't be sure of the exact time, but he did know that Rachel was in his arms, naked to the waist, her breasts pressed to his chest. Arousal, hot and urgent, sealed them together.

"What happened?"

"Later," he muttered as he brought his mouth back to hers for a frantic kiss.

He'd never wanted a woman more. Never needed this woman more. And she must have agreed, because her mouth began to move against his with urgency.

He felt as if he were drowning, with no one to save him except Rachel.

Perhaps she was feeling the same thing, because she made a hungry sound and slid her arms around his neck. Her lips never leaving his, she deepened the kiss.

He had wanted her since they'd first come here and all the way through the scene in the clinic.

Now he felt his heart slamming against the inside of his chest as he gathered her to him.

He was lost in the taste of her, the feel of her mouth on his. They had traveled on an extraordinary journey, but his only reality was the warm, pliant woman in his arms.

And he heard her thoughts echoing his.

It was the same for her. The very same.

When her hands slid to his hips, and she pulled him to her, rocking her body against the rigid flesh behind his fly, he thought he would go out of his mind.

Then her hands were at the button of his jeans. When she'd opened it, she began lowering the zipper.

Exactly what he'd been silently begging her to do.

And he did the same for her, helping her shuck off the

jeans that had kept them from making love before their strange journey.

He wanted her with a physical need that bordered on madness, but that was only a small part of what he felt for her.

With her he could have all the things he'd always craved. Things he had never allowed himself to put into words.

Because he still could hardly believe them, he focused on the physical. He wanted to arouse her slowly, to enjoy every moment of her pleasure before he took anything for himself.

He caressed her from shoulder to hip, enjoying the feel of his hand sliding over her silky skin and the feel of her body stirring under his touch.

Delicately he stroked the inner curve of one breast, then the other, gratified when he heard her breath catch and then quicken for him.

She liked what he was doing. He knew that from her physical response and from her thoughts. Still, he caught her frustration and realized she wasn't going to let him slow them down.

Before he could do anything about it, she had pushed him to his back and climbed on top of him, bringing him inside her. She hardly waited for the two of them to absorb that sensation before she began to move, setting a frantic rhythm that pushed them toward a blazing climax that flashed through them like strokes of lightning.

He felt her contract around him, felt her pleasure wash over him, felt more than he had ever felt possible.

Then she collapsed on top of him in a damp heap, and they clung together.

He wrapped his arms around her as they lay panting on the bed. Neither of them had to ask if it had been good. They both *knew*.

He closed his eyes, stroking his lips against her cheek.

Did you ever travel in time like that before?

Never. You?

No.

Why was Evelyn Morgan there?

I don't know.

Is that how she knew us? She'd seen us before.

He thought about that. *She was younger. We were in her past, but she was seeing us the way we are now.*

But did she remember that when she came to New Orleans to find us?

Again, there was no sure answer.

We could have warned her.

About something that was going to happen a quarter century later?

She made a rough sound. *I guess you're right.*

We had to get away.

She nodded against his shoulder.

When he started to sit up, she kept her hand on his arm. *Stay with me for a while.*

He lay back down and tried to relax, but he knew she felt his tension—mental and physical.

Finally she rolled to her side. *Okay. Go check your computer.*

Sorry.

No, you're right. We can't just stay here enjoying ourselves. We have to figure out where the Solomon Clinic is.

He got up and got the laptop that he'd brought. When he turned back, he saw her straightening the bed.

Setting the computer down again, he helped her pull up the sheet, blanket and spread.

As she reached for her bra and panties, he stifled his impulse to stop her.

Modesty.

Less fun.

More focus on business.

As a concession to that idea, he pulled on his briefs before punching up the pillow and climbing back into bed.

Rachel moved beside him so she could see the screen while he did a Google search.

He put in the date he thought was right for their visit, then the Solomon Clinic and the Waterside Restaurant.

In seconds the search engine had come back with the name of a town.

Houma, Louisiana.

They looked at each other.

"Not too far from here. I guess you were right about which direction to head in." He checked a little further. "The Waterside Restaurant's still there." It had a website, and he clicked on a picture of the deck out back, which didn't look too different from when they'd seen it before, although the furniture had been updated.

"Maybe we can get some crawfish étouffée. And some information."

Maybe we have to be cautious. Eric Smithson might be waiting in town, hoping we'll show up.

How would he know we'd go there?

If he knows about the place, he might assume we'd be trying to find out about it. But we have to take that chance.

He moved restlessly on the bed. "I'd like to flush him out—if he's there."

"After we get a little sleep," she countered.

"Are you stalling?"

"You know I am. But I'm also exhausted. It's not a good idea to go into a situation that could be dangerous when we're not at our best."

He took her point. He was also grappling with the impulse to drive right past Houma and keep going, but he had the feeling they would never be safe if they kept running. And he knew from her churning thoughts that she agreed.

Despite his eagerness to get the search over with, he settled down beside her on the bed.

He'd thought he was too keyed up to sleep, but maybe time travel took a lot of energy.

They were both asleep within minutes and stayed that way for several hours.

And she was right. When he woke up, he was feeling better able to cope with whatever was in Houma.

While Rachel took a shower, he did some more research on Houma.

"What do we know about the place?" Rachel asked when she came out of the bathroom.

"The population is around one hundred twenty-five thousand. You can book swamp tours and fishing expeditions, eat spicy Cajun food, walk bird trails in the wildlife park."

"It's not all that large."

"But it has a long history and a historic downtown area. The Terrebonne Parish Courthouse is located there."

"No mention of a Solomon Clinic?"

"No."

"Maybe we should change our appearance before we go there," she said.

"You mean more than a change of clothing."

"Yeah. As you pointed out, it's a small place. I don't want to be recognized."

They stopped at a big-box shopping mall where he told her to see if she could find a blond wig. Meanwhile, he bought work boots, a cowboy hat and a denim shirt, which he tore the sleeves off of and wore open down the front.

"Nice," she murmured when she saw him.

"So are you," he answered, taking in the wig.

"You like me as a blonde?"

She answered her own question. *Don't bother to lie. I'll get rid of the damn thing as soon as I can.*

They both put on sunglasses as they drove away from the shopping center.

They stopped for burgers, which they ate as they drove toward the town.

He'd looked at some pictures on the web, but it was a strange experience driving into Houma.

"Do you recognize anything?" she asked after they'd entered the city limits.

"I'm not sure. Maybe I have some vague memory of coming to a place like this, but it has to have changed over the years."

The area was bounded by rivers and bayous. They had to cross a bridge to get into town and another soon after. They headed for the downtown area. As they drove past art galleries, T-shirt shops and restaurants, they kept an eye out for the man who had tried to take them captive twice.

Finally they passed the Waterside Restaurant.

"In our...vision...we came down the street from the Solomon Clinic," Rachel said. "It was only a few doors away.

"The restaurant's still here." She gestured toward what she thought was the location of the clinic. "But that building doesn't look like what we saw. Does it to you?"

"No." He eyed the structure. "It looks like newer construction."

"They must have torn the place down."

He made a rough sound. "Maybe they thought it was haunted."

"Or something." After a long moment, Rachel cleared her throat.

Before she could speak, Jake said, "You're right."

"What are you, a mind reader or something?"

She laughed, and he went on.

"The clinic's gone, and we're not going to find out anything unless we start asking some questions."

"But where should we start?"

"Maybe a casual conversation in a restaurant."

They stopped at a place called Big Ralph's, where the decor was simple and rustic, and a sign told them to seat themselves.

After they'd claimed a wooden booth in the back, a short, plump woman who looked to be in her fifties came over to take their order. Her name tag identified her as Maddie.

By mutual agreement, Rachel was the one who struck up a conversation. "We'd just like a snack. What do you recommend?"

"The shrimp gumbo is excellent."

Rachel looked at Jake. "We could each have a bowl."

"Sounds good to me."

"And sweetened iced tea."

After they'd placed their order, Jake sat back and stretched out his legs.

When the waitress brought the tea, he said, "So what do you recommend for someone with a few days in town?"

"Do you like to fish?"

"Uh-huh. Do you have nature walks?" Rachel asked.

"Sure do. You can pick up some brochures by the door."

"What about a bed-and-breakfast with cottages?"

She thought for a moment. "The Magnolia House would be perfect. It's very charming. Mrs. Madison runs the place and cooks wonderful breakfasts. Do you want me to call and find out if they have a cottage available?"

"That would be very nice of you, but we don't want you to go to any trouble."

"No trouble at all."

"Then thanks so much," Rachel answered.

The woman was back with their gumbo and a smile on her face in a few minutes. "Mrs. Madison is holding a cottage for you," she said as she set down their bowls. She also had a slip of paper with the address and phone number of the B&B.

"We'll go over as soon as we finish eating," Jake said.

Rachel set down her spoon. "I'm a history buff. I was looking at the history of the town, and I came across a place called the Solomon Clinic."

Jake saw the waitress stiffen.

"The Solomon Clinic," she said slowly. "How did you hear about that?"

"It came up when I was talking to a woman who said she'd been there as a child."

"It's closed," the waitress said, her voice turning icy.

"I see."

"It wasn't one of the scenic attractions in town."

"What did they do there?"

"I really don't know." The waitress turned away abruptly and left the table.

That question certainly got a reaction.

Uh-huh.

The place must have had some kind of bad reputation.

We'll check into the Magnolia House, then ask around some more.

Is that a good idea?

What do you suggest?

Perusing old newspapers.

Okay.

As soon as they'd finished their gumbo, the waitress was back with the check. Her smile was gone, and she didn't have any more conversational gambits.

Jake paid in cash, and they left quickly.

In the car he said, "We'll use the name on my alternate credit card. Mr. and Mrs. Jack Le Barron."

"Okay." She sighed. "What's my name?"

He thought for a moment. "It should start with the same letter. What about Reagan?"

Jake consulted the address, then stopped at a gas station to ask directions. The Magnolia House bed-and-breakfast was located outside of town on a wooded tract off the main road.

Fifteen minutes later, they found a sign advertising the establishment and turned in at an access road through stands of oak and cypress trees.

Up ahead was a circular driveway in front of a red brick mansion with a portico and white columns out front.

"This really is lovely," Rachel murmured.

Jake nodded. He didn't particularly care about the accommodations, but if a nice room made a difference to Rachel, he didn't mind.

Thanks.

He was still disconcerted to discover that what was intended as a private thought was being picked up by someone else.

She didn't comment on that as they climbed out of the car and started toward the sign that said Office.

Before they reached the door, a woman came hurrying out. She looked to be in her sixties, with short salt-and-pepper hair, large brown eyes and a worried expression.

"Did Maddie from Big Ralph's send you over?"

"Yes," Rachel answered.

"I'm so sorry, but she was mistaken. I don't have a cottage to rent—or anything in the main house, either."

Jake stared at her, wishing he had the ability to read more than Rachel's mind.

Figuring he had nothing to lose, he said, "Are you turning us away because we were interested in the Solomon Clinic?"

She blanched. "We don't like to talk about that place."

"Why not?"

"I'd prefer not to continue the topic."

Before he could say anything else, she turned and hustled back into the office.

They stood staring after her.

"Well, that was…something," Rachel murmured as she stared at the doorway through which Mrs. Madison had disappeared.

He reached for her hand. "I'm sorry. I know you were looking forward to staying somewhere charming."

"It's not that important."

Of course, he didn't believe her. They'd been under a lot of pressure, and she'd wanted to enjoy some of the town ambience, but neither one of them wanted to continue the discussion.

As they drove away, she made a quick change of subject. "Do you think the clinic was unpopular here? Or is there a conspiracy to protect it?"

"It could be either. Or both."

"Is there a library in town?"

"I think we passed one. I guess we'd better stop bringing up the subject with residents and just stick with newspaper files."

"We have no idea what we're looking for. Or even what year," Rachel said.

"We know it was in existence when we were here…" He stopped and thought about himself and Rachel as they'd been when they'd seen the children. "At least when we were three or four or five. Can you think of any other clues?"

"Could we go back there instead of the library? I mean, to the building that's sitting where the clinic used to be."

"Sure." He turned the car around and headed back to the downtown area, then found the Waterside Restaurant again and pulled a few doors down to where they thought the clinic would have been.

"I'm getting out," Rachel said.

"Wait a minute. What do you expect to find?"

"I don't know, but I have the feeling that I'll pick up something."

"Do you need me with you?"

"Let me try it alone. So you don't have to find a parking space down here."

He looked around and didn't see anyone obviously watching them, but what if that Smithson guy had come to town and was waiting for them at this spot? The thought made his stomach knot.

I don't think he's here, she reassured him as she headed for the building that stood on the old clinic site. After looking up and down the street again, she reached to press her palm against the brick exterior.

For long moments, her expression didn't change. Then she closed her eyes.

And he heard her gasp.

Chapter Fourteen

Jake was about to scramble out of the car, when Rachel came running back and climbed into the passenger seat.

"What was that?" he asked as he lurched away from the curb.

"It burned."

"What burned? What are you talking about?"

She put her hand on his arm, pressing her fingers into his flesh as she sent him a vivid picture of the clinic building as they'd seen it earlier.

Flames leaped through the waiting room, caught the draperies, climbed up the walls. As he stared at the awful scene, he had the same shocked reaction that she had. They'd been in that room!

The flames interfered with his vision, and he pulled into the parking lot of a bank where he sat behind the wheel, breathing hard.

"Sorry," she whispered.

"It's okay." He threw his head back, leaning against the seat. "At least the waiting room was empty."

"Thank the Lord. I think the fire took place at night."

"What happened? Was it an accident?"

"No."

He turned to her questioningly.

"I saw that part, too. Do you want to see?"

"Yeah."

She kept her hand on his arm and sent him another picture—that of a shadowy figure, with a stocking mask over his face, moving through the waiting room. Because it was dark, it was hard to see clearly, but Jake could tell that the man was holding a can of gasoline and sloshing it onto the floor and furnishings. Then he walked through a door and into the back of the clinic. Rachel stayed with him as he walked past examination rooms and offices, continuing to spread the gasoline around.

When he reached an exit, he pushed it open and stepped out into an alley where he struck a match and tossed it inside. He stood for a moment, watching the flames spring up, then he closed the door and walked away down the alley.

"Who was he?" Jake asked, thinking there was something familiar about him, but he couldn't put his finger on what it was.

Rachel's brow wrinkled. "It was hard to tell with his face covered."

Jake shifted in his seat. "When did it burn?"

She shrugged.

"There should be some way to find out."

He pulled out of the parking lot and headed back the way they'd come, then found a coffee shop with wireless network. While he got a table, Rachel ordered them both medium-size lattes.

When she came back with the drinks and set them on the table, he gestured for her to move her chair around to his side of the table where she could see the screen.

"I had enough information to get a date," he said, careful to reveal nothing aloud that other patrons might overhear.

She looked at the news article he'd found. "That's a few years after we were there, I think."

"That sounds right."

She quickly read the article, which said that the Solomon Clinic in Houma, Louisiana, had burned one night. Although the fire was judged arson, there was no indication who had done it.

Jake watched her face when she came to the surprising piece of information that he'd already seen.

It was a fertility clinic! Not some place where they were running medical experiments.

Yeah. A fertility clinic, run by a doctor Douglas Solomon. He leaned back and took a sip of the latte. *So it was a place where couples came who were having trouble conceiving a child.*

She nodded, a faraway look in her eyes.

He didn't have to ask what she was thinking because he was able to follow along.

My mother told me that she had a hard time getting pregnant. She told me she had expensive treatments.

And she made you feel guilty about that because you weren't more...loving.

Rachel sighed. *I tried.*

He reached across the table and took her hand.

We're getting off the subject. I guess my parents must have been there for the same reason if we both ended up at that clinic.

What kind of techniques were they using?

He shrugged. *You say it was your mother who couldn't conceive?*

I don't know that for sure.

What else did she say?

Not a lot. I think she was always embarrassed about it— like she'd been a failure when it came to something that should be natural.

Jake kept scanning the article, then raised his head.

It says here they were using in vitro fertilization. Where the sperm and egg meet in a petri dish.

Why would people be afraid to talk about the clinic so long after it burned down?

There must be some other factor.

It could have been an issue in town. Some people might not have approved of tampering with God's will.

That's possible. Or the clinic was questioned for other reasons. He leaned back, thinking, and knew she had followed his silent question.

Why did they make the kids go back, over and over? she asked.

You remember having tests?

Like IQ tests?

Yeah.

They both considered various explanations.

I mean, what if he wanted a lot of fertilized eggs to experiment on?

They were both silent for long moments.

And do what?

To create telepaths? he finally asked. *But would anyone have thought of that so long ago?*

Or even now.

True.

If we had a bunch of IQ tests, it sounds like it had something to do with brain function. Maybe this doctor had some other effect in mind, and he didn't know the ultimate result?

Jake went back to the computer, until he was interrupted by a powerful thought from Rachel.

It was her. I mean the guy who set the fire.

He turned around and stared at her.

Rachel went on, her excited thoughts coming out in a fast stream. *It looked like a man with a mask, but Evelyn Morgan was the one sloshing the gasoline around the clinic. Evelyn.*

Jake brought back the picture Rachel had sent him. They'd both thought it was a guy, but someone short and slender—who could have actually been a woman.

I thought there was something familiar about the arsonist. The limp. You remember her limp?

Yes, but why was she burning the place down?

To hide evidence, Rachel answered immediately. *More reason to think the in vitro fertilization was a cover for something else.*

They both sat silently, mulling that over, but they were unable to come to any conclusions.

We made some assumptions about Evelyn that might not be true.

She wasn't such a sweet old lady.

Back when she burned the clinic, maybe she had job to do—and she followed orders.

Jake went back to the computer, looking for more information on the fire.

He found another article that quoted a nurse who worked there, saying that it was fortunate the fire had been at night so that no parents and children had been injured.

"Maven Bolton," Rachel said the nurse's name aloud.

"Maybe she's still in town." Jake went to one of the search engines and found a listing in Houma for a woman with that name.

"You think it's the same person?"

He did some more digging. "She's a retired nurse. She worked at the local hospital for fifteen years. It says she was at a private clinic before that."

"So what are we going to say to her?"

He thought for a moment. *That...after my parents died, I found some information about the Solomon Clinic, and wanted to talk to someone who had worked there.*

And who am I?

My fiancée. You wanted to come with me.

Although she nodded, he knew she was unsure.

It'll be safer for us—and her—if we don't tell her anything more.

She sighed. *You're right.*

As they left the coffee shop, Jake checked the area again but didn't see anyone paying attention to them. Still, he couldn't shake the feeling that they were going to run into trouble—sooner rather than later.

Beside him, Rachel shivered, and he reached for her hand and squeezed.

Sorry.

He responded to her unspoken thought. *You're right. Something bad is coming.*

They drove to the address he'd found, which turned out to be a one-story red brick building that was an extended-care facility for the elderly.

"I hope her memory's all right," Rachel said as they pulled into the parking lot, and Jake cut the engine.

They walked up a path through nicely landscaped grounds where native plants were interspersed with beds of colorful flowers.

Double doors led to a reception area, where an efficient-looking young woman was sitting behind a desk. She was wearing a name tag that identified her as Sarah Dalton.

"Can I help you?" she asked.

"We'd like to visit with Maven Bolton."

"Are you relatives?"

"No. We're old friends," Jake said. "We were passing through town, and we thought we'd drop in on Maven."

"She doesn't get too many visitors. I'm sure she'll be pleased to see you," Ms. Dalton said, standing up and checking her watch. "Maven should be in the dayroom now."

They followed the woman down a hallway, and Jake noted

that as senior residences went, it wasn't too bad. It looked clean, and he didn't detect any unwanted smells.

Rachel gave him a sideways glance, and he shrugged as they stepped into a large, sunny room. Potted plants were arranged around the walls.

A lot of old women and a few old men were sitting around the room. Some were in wheelchairs, others in easy chairs, watching television or at tables playing cards or working puzzles.

The employee led them to a woman who was sitting by the window with a magazine in her lap. She had short gray hair and a wrinkled face, but she was wearing a nice-looking flowered blouse and tan slacks.

"Some people to see you, Maven," Ms. Dalton said.

The nursing home resident looked up inquiringly.

"It's been a long time," Jake said. "I'm Jack Le Barron. And this is my fiancée, Reagan…" He paused for a moment, realizing that he hadn't thought of another last name for Rachel.

"West," she supplied.

Maven nodded, probably trying to place him, but to his relief, Ms. Dalton turned and headed back toward the front of the building.

"Thank you for seeing us," Rachel said.

"I don't remember you," she said in a tentative voice.

"That's all right."

"It isn't!" the old woman objected.

Rachel and Jake both pulled up chairs and sat down. "We don't want to bother you, but we'd like some information, if you have the time."

"What kind of information?"

Jake glanced at Rachel, then said, "My parents had trouble conceiving me, and I didn't want to run into the same problem when we get married."

The old woman looked wary.

"I think my parents went to a fertility clinic in town," Jake continued.

"It's been closed for years."

"You worked there?"

Her face tightened.

"You were quoted in a newspaper article about the place when there was a fire," Rachel said gently.

Maven looked away from her.

"The Solomon Clinic," Rachel prompted.

The woman's lips compressed. "Dr. Solomon doesn't like us to talk about it. He might get angry with me."

"He's still alive?" Jake asked.

Her gaze darted away from them. "I shouldn't be talking about it."

When she folded her arms across her chest, Jake continued in a soothing voice, "The clinic did a lot of good work, helping childless couples."

"Yes," Maven murmured.

"But they were doing something else, too," Rachel said.

Maven shook her head vigorously. "We're not supposed to talk about that."

"Okay."

The woman looked agitated and lowered her voice. "Don't tell Dr. Solomon that I said anything."

"Of course we won't."

The woman's expression turned secretive, and she lowered her voice. "He wanted to make smarter children. That's a noble goal, isn't it?"

"What?" Rachel asked.

"Smarter children." The old woman's expression changed abruptly. "I want you to leave now," she said.

Rachel and Jake glanced at each other. They'd just confirmed one of their speculations, and they both wanted to keep pressing her.

"I'm already in trouble. Please leave," she said.

Some of the other residents were looking at them. Which was probably their cue to leave.

They both stood. "Thank you for your time," Jake said. "It means a lot to us."

Maven nodded tightly, then looked down at the magazine in her lap.

They both walked toward the door, then into the hall.

She's afraid, Rachel said.

Was she warned not to talk, or is she trying to protect her role at the clinic?

There's no way of knowing. But we do know what the clinic was doing. Trying to increase the intelligence of the children conceived there.

If it's the truth, Jake answered.

It makes sense—with all that IQ testing. She stopped and thought for a moment. *But wouldn't all that be illegal?*

He answered with a mirthless laugh. *The government and private research groups have done a lot of things that are illegal—or stupid—in the name of experimentation. You've heard about soldiers lined up to watch nuclear explosions. Or doctors who deliberately didn't treat a bunch of black men with syphilis to find out what would happen to them. Somebody paid a lot of money to fund Dr. Solomon's research. Would a small-town doctor have those kinds of resources? I think we have to assume someone with deeper pockets was footing the bill. The government or a pharmaceutical company, maybe. But I think they were dissatisfied with the results. I mean, back when Solomon had a working clinic. Maybe they sent Evelyn Morgan to check on the doctor's progress. And she reported that there wasn't anything unusual about the children's intelligence. The experiment was a big failure.*

And when her boss didn't like what she found out, he told her to burn the place down, Rachel added. *Which is kind of extreme, don't you think?*

Apparently he's an extreme kind of guy. He didn't just come asking you or me questions. He sent a thug after us. Probably to find out what he could before killing us.

Rachel winced. *But that still leaves us with one big question—why did Evelyn try to get us together?*

Suppose she researched children from the clinic and thought they might have developed some kind of special talent when they were paired up?

Of course, there's another question, Rachel said. *We don't know if Dr. Solomon is really alive. He could have died years ago, and Maven's not remembering correctly. Or he could be nearby, keeping an ear out for anyone who talks about the clinic. And then what?*

Jake shrugged. *It could even be that people have heard about Evelyn's death, and that's got them worried.*

Rachel nodded. *Do we look for Dr. Solomon?*

That could be dangerous.

As they walked past the front desk, Jake nodded to Ms. Dalton. "Thank you."

"Did you have a nice visit?"

"Yes." He waited a beat before asking, "Is Maven often confused?"

"Sometimes her memory is a little shaky."

"Thanks," he said again.

In the parking lot, he started the car but didn't immediately drive away. "We have to find a place to stay," he said.

"And this time, we don't mention anything about the Solomon Clinic."

"Unless word about us has already spread around town."

She worried her bottom lip between her teeth. "You think people are talking about the nosy couple asking questions?"

"No. It was just my frustration coming out."

They drove away from the facility and headed toward the downtown area. They'd just passed the site of the old clinic when Jake made an angry sound as he focused on a man sitting in a car in the bank parking lot.

Rachel stiffened. "It's him. Smithson. The guy from New Orleans. He's found us."

"Yeah."

"And we've got to do something about it." Rachel's brow furrowed. "Let me think. What about—"

He didn't let her finish. "No."

"You've got a better idea?"

His expression turned grim. "No."

As he pulled out of the parking lot, Jake took evasive action, driving down a few side streets, then checked his rearview mirror to make sure he had no tail before heading toward the highway.

He passed a couple of large motel chains, then pointed toward a sign that said Cabins.

"Probably not as nice as that fancy place, but we need some privacy."

She nodded.

They drove a short distance up a gravel road hemmed in by cypress trees dripping with Spanish moss where they found a rustic building with an Office sign out front.

Jake parked under a tree with low-hanging branches.

Without being told what to do, Rachel scrunched down in her seat and waited while Jake went in.

Inside he found an old guy wearing a pair of faded overalls.

"Help you?"

Jake affected a thick drawl. "My honey and I need a room for the night."

"Sure."

He paid in cash and gave a false license-plate number on the registration form.

When the guy reached for a key, Jake asked, "You got a real private cabin?"

"They're all off by theirselves."

"Appreciate the privacy."

"Okay. Number four, then. You go up to the end of the road till you can't drive no farther."

"Thanks."

Jake returned to the car and drove down the road, deeper into what looked like a wilderness area.

He could see some cabins through the foliage, but kept going until he reached the end of the road, where he found a small shingled building with a parking area in front. Behind it he could see a slow-moving bayou.

After he pulled up in front, they both got out and looked around.

"I guess this is as private as we can expect," Rachel said, and he heard the quaver in her voice. "It looks like the setting for a slasher movie."

Jake reached for her hand and knit his fingers with hers.

"We don't have to stay here," he said. "We don't even have to stay in town."

"I want to."

He knew she wasn't exactly telling the truth, but he didn't challenge her as he crossed the porch and opened the door to the modest unit.

When they stepped inside the cabin, he looked around at the rustic furnishings.

"Early pioneer."

She laughed nervously.

As he reached for her, she came into his arms, and they clung to each other.

"Is it ever going to get any better?" she murmured.

"Yes," he answered with as much conviction as he could muster.

"You're sure?"

"I'll make sure."

She clung to him for a moment longer before easing away. "I want to take off this damn blond wig."

"You don't think blondes have more fun?"

"Not so far." She pulled off the wig and spent a few moments combing her dark hair so that it fell in waves around her shoulders.

When she caught Jake watching her, she said, "We should practice communicating when we're not touching."

He nodded. "And when we can't see each other."

"As many barriers as possible. You should leave me alone here."

Fear leaped inside him. "Not yet."

When she walked into the bathroom and closed the door, he retreated to the wall near the door. After looking out the window to make sure no one had followed them, he leaned his shoulder against the wall and reached for her with his mind.

It was getting easier. He got a sense of her fairly quickly, but her thoughts weren't clear to him. However, he didn't give up, and soon he was picking up flickers from her mind.

He wanted to send her a strong message—of hope and promise.

I love you.

He felt joy leap within her. *I'm never going to get tired of hearing that. I don't know how I lived without you.*

Same here. And now we have to make sure that we're left in peace to live our lives.

What would you do if you were free to do anything you wanted?

Pick up my life where I left off. My shop and my business.

You were lonely.

But everything's changed, now that I have you.

There are a lot of impediments to going back to life in the city.

We have to be patient!

They stayed for a few more minutes, speaking to each other, mind to mind. And practicing some of the skills they'd recently learned.

He focused on the television, willing it to come on, and felt Rachel joining him in the effort. After several seconds, the screen flickered to life, and he pumped his hand into the air.

"All right!"

Keep it up, tiger.

He grinned. *I can't do it without you.*

Glad to be of service, but can we do something a little harder?

Like what?

I'd try to start a fire or something, but I don't think the management would appreciate it if we burned this place down.

Finally, he knew they were just stalling. *I'm going out to get some dinner,* he said. *What do you want?*

Not something from Ralph's. Something fast.

She came out of the bathroom and walked into his arms. He folded her close. Things were moving rapidly, and it was hard not to consider that this might be the last time they embraced each other. He tried to keep his mind away from those dark thoughts, but he knew she picked them up.

Needing to reassure himself—and her as well—he brought his mouth to hers for a kiss that he intended to be warm and gentle. It quickly turned hot and urgent. His mouth moved over hers as he tried to show how much he needed her, how much he wanted her.

They were both breathing hard when he finally tore his mouth away.

"I'd better get out of here while the getting's good," he gasped.

"We'll take up where we left off when you get back," she whispered.

"It's a date." He dragged in a breath and let it out. "You're sure you're up for staying alone?"

"No. But it makes sense."

Before he lost the will to leave, he walked out the door and closed it behind him.

Outside, he kept up the communication with her.

You're still here.

He walked slowly to the car, feeling the link between them stretch. By the time he'd got in, he had lost the contact, which gave him a jittery feeling, along with a profound sense of loss. With his teeth clenched, he pulled away from the space in front of their cabin and headed up the gravel road. When he reached the highway, he turned toward the row of fast-food restaurants that he'd seen earlier. But his mind was spinning, calculating the time he would be away from Rachel.

RACHEL HAD TRIED TO PUT on a brave face while Jake had been here. And she knew she had partially succeeded in keeping him from overhearing her darkest thoughts. Now that she was alone in this dingy cabin, it was impossible to keep up the act. When her knees felt weak, she sat down in the lumpy easy chair and gripped the arms.

"Stop it," she muttered to herself. "You volunteered to stay here."

Which could have been a big mistake. Still, she willed herself to steadiness. When she was feeling calmer, she got up and went into the bathroom, where she splashed cold water on her face.

Out in the bedroom again, she peered through the window. It was dark under the trees, making the landscape look spooky. She hated being so alone and isolated, but as far as she could see, there was no alternative.

The seconds ticked by, and she tried to reach out to Jake. He was much too far away, and she couldn't locate him at all. It was as if he didn't exist.

But he would be back soon.

Her shoulders were so tight that she was starting to give herself a headache.

Again, she reached toward Jake and found nothing. This time, she couldn't stop a spurt of fear from slicing through her.

What if they'd gotten it all wrong? What if Eric Smithson came after him while he was picking up dinner? That might make sense. If the stalker disabled the man, he'd have free rein with the woman.

As a graphic image leaped into her head, she shuddered and started pacing the room again.

Did she hear footsteps outside? She wanted to look out the window, but that would only expose her to view if the guy was skulking around outside.

When the doorknob rattled, she jumped. Her heart began to pound as she sent her mind to the other side of the barrier, searching for Jake, even when she was pretty sure she wasn't going to find him there.

Instead, the door burst open. Smithson crashed into the room and advanced on her, gun in hand.

Before she could scream, he clamped a hand over her mouth.

Chapter Fifteen

"Thanks for picking such a nice private location. This time you're going to tell me what I want to know."

Rachel tried to contain her fear, but she felt herself trembling in his grip.

"Come on. We're getting out of here before your boyfriend gets back."

"No, please," she tried to plead, but it was only a muffled gasp.

"There's something going on with you two, and I *will* find out what the hell it is."

Just as he had at her shop in New Orleans, he'd come prepared with handcuffs, which he pulled out of his pocket. "If you scream, I'll bash these across your face. Do you understand?"

She nodded.

He took his hand off her mouth.

"Put the cuffs on."

With no alternative, she clicked first one cuff around her wrist, then the other. But at least her hands were in front of her.

"Why are you after us?" she gasped out.

"The Badger wants to know what you're up to. But it's more than that."

"The Badger. That's a person?" she asked, struggling with her own confusion.

"You're not the one asking questions," he retorted as he grabbed her arm.

She could try to fight him with her mind, but she knew it wouldn't do much good, not with Jake gone. He'd managed to generate a thunderbolt alone, but it hadn't had much power. And she'd only done it with his help.

She tried to send a desperate message to him, but it was as though she were flinging her thoughts into a fast-running river, where they were swept away.

When the man hustled her toward the door, she dug her heels into the rug, but he pulled her along, his fingers making marks on her arm.

Panic shot through her as they stepped outside, and he began marching her toward a car parked in front of the cabin. Oh, Lord, this wasn't supposed to happen.

She looked wildly around and saw no one and no other cars. Apparently nobody was near this section of the grounds, which meant screaming for help would do her no good.

Still, in desperation, she silently cried out.

Jake, Jake, he's got me. Please get here in time.

When he didn't answer, she knew she was going to have to try something herself.

"Come on."

The man pulled at her arm, hustling her toward the car.

If he got her in there, she knew she was dead. Just like Evelyn Morgan. Dragging her feet, she struggled to summon up mental energy. As he yanked the car door open, she sucked in her will and hit him with a bolt of power.

He staggered back.

"What the hell?"

Instead of replying, she ran. She got partway across the

parking lot when the kidnapper caught up with her and clamped a hand on her arm.

As she tried to summon another energy bolt, he slapped her across the face so hard that she almost blacked out.

When she fell, she felt him catch her under the arms and drag her toward the car. By the time they reached it, she had recovered enough to stiffen her arm and make her body rigid as he tried to push her through the door.

When he socked her between the shoulder blades, she lost her grip on the door frame and fell into the backseat, but she wasn't going to give up yet.

Whipping around, she kicked out, her feet hitting him somewhere in his midsection.

"Bitch," he growled in anger, coming at her again, but her head had cleared enough for her to gather some strength to send another feeble energy bolt at him.

Probably it wasn't much worse than a bee sting, but as it struck him, his curse filled the car's interior.

"What the hell are you doing?"

She didn't waste energy answering.

But he apparently was too incensed now to think clearly. He lunged at her, coming down on top of her, closing his hands around her throat.

She tried to drag in a breath, but there was nothing there. Panic gripped her. Spots danced behind her eyes as she struggled to hold on to consciousness. Was this how it would end?

Smithson cursed, eased up on the pressure.

"Got to question you," he growled.

Her moan almost drowned out a sound that came to her from far away. Tires on gravel.

And inside her head, Jake's desperate question.

Rachel, Rachel, are you all right?

She tried to answer, but her brain was too fogged.

Jake's feet made the gravel fly as he charged toward them.

But apparently her attacker figured out it wasn't just the woman and him anymore. He lurched out of the car, going for the gun he had stuck in the waistband of his jeans.

With Smithson's hands gone from her throat, Rachel dragged in a breath. Even as she started coughing, she kicked his hand, sending the gun flying into the parking lot.

The guy cursed, but now Rachel's attention was on Jake, as his eyes flashed to her.

Can you help me? he asked.

Yes.

Everything happened very fast then.

Jake didn't have to tell her what to do. Still coughing, she let him direct the process, feeling a ball of power form in his mind. Even in her weakened state, she was able to add to it, sensing it grow and build. Jake flung it from him, slamming it into the man who had tried to kidnap her.

He staggered back, hitting the wall of the cabin, and she climbed out of the car as Jake launched another blast of energy that propelled the man backward through the doorway.

Jake leaped forward, grabbing the assailant by the collar, hauling him up and slamming a fist into his face, and she knew that he'd needed the physical impact, not just the mental one.

As the guy went limp, Jake looked around the parking area, making sure that no one had been watching them.

Desperate to free herself from her shackles, Rachel knelt beside the kidnapper and fumbled in his pocket for the handcuff key, which she extracted and tried to fit into the lock.

But it was hard to work with her wrists cuffed together. Jake helped her, and they pulled the restraints off her wrists, then clicked them onto Smithson. When he started to stir, Jake socked him again.

Together they hauled him into the cabin, across the carpet and onto the bed, attaching the handcuffs to a bedpost.

"Be right back."

Jake charged into the parking lot again, heading for the guy's car. When he returned, he was carrying a length of rope. Quickly they tied the attacker's feet to the end of the bed so that he was pinned down at his wrists and ankles.

When he opened his eyes and started to buck, Jake gave him a piece of advice. "Settle down, if you don't want to get hurt—very badly."

The guy gave them a murderous look but stopped struggling.

Jake turned away and pulled Rachel into his arms. "Are you all right?"

"Yes."

They switched to silent communication.

I'm so sorry, Jake said.

It was my idea. Making him think I was defenseless.

Yeah, but it put you in too much danger.

I don't think either one of us was quite prepared for how it went down, she answered. *Let's not play the blame game. We've got work to do.*

But he still couldn't let it go. *I got stopped at a traffic light on the way back. I didn't know if I'd get here in time.*

You did.

But he almost had you in the car.

I would have kept pounding him with my mind.

If you'd still been conscious. Thank God you're okay.

He hugged her tightly, and she clung to him, thankful that he'd gotten back in time.

Finally, she turned to the man on the bed.

"You're going to give us some answers."

"Like hell."

"I suppose you're prepared to hold up under torture."

Even tied down, the guy was defiant. "Try and make me talk. See where it gets you."

Jake shrugged. "Yeah, we'll see."

"When he thought he was getting me out of here, he told me he worked for someone named the Badger," Rachel volunteered.

The guy grimaced. "Fat lot of good that will do you."

"And what's your real name?" Jake asked.

The man clamped his lips together.

"He said there was something strange about us," Rachel murmured.

I guess he's going to find out what it is, Jake answered.

Let me see what I can do, Rachel suggested. She felt Jake mentally step back, allowing her to direct the process as she probed the man's mind.

The guy's face contorted as he felt her mental fingers walking through his brain.

"You're doing it again," he shouted.

Ignoring him, Rachel dug for information.

"You're not Eric Smithson. Your real name is Carter Frederick," she said after several seconds.

His eyes widened. "What did you just do?"

"What Dr. Solomon made it possible for us to do," she answered, watching his face.

He reacted to the name.

Getting Frederick's name hadn't been all that difficult, but extracting more information wasn't so simple. The guy who called himself the Badger had taken the code name to stay anonymous. From their business conversations, all Carter Frederick knew was that the man who'd hired him had been some high muck-a-muck in Washington. He'd moved somewhere out West, but Frederick didn't know where.

Rachel rummaged around in the man's head, not sure exactly what she was doing. But one clear memory stood out.

"You killed Evelyn Morgan," she breathed.

"No."

"You're lying."

He gave her a defiant look. "You can't prove anything."

Could they?

Maybe if Frederick had been in better shape, he might have resisted. But the recent information in his brain was theirs for the taking. She saw the scene in Evelyn Morgan's hotel room. The woman had opened the door, and Frederick had burst in.

He'd tied her up, started asking questions and gotten rough when he didn't get what he wanted.

She'd lashed out at him with her legs, then made a dash for the door. But Frederick had caught up with her, and she'd hit her head on the radiator while trying to get away.

Rachel felt sick as she leaned against Jake.

She glanced at Carter Frederick, who was lying on the bed with his eyes closed, his breath shallow. "I want to get away from this disgusting piece of work."

"Let's go outside."

After Jake checked to make sure there was no chance of Frederick's escaping, they stepped onto the covered porch and walked across the gravel parking area, to where a picnic table sat under some shade trees.

"What are we going to do with him?" Rachel whispered when they had both sat down.

Jake shook his head. "I haven't gotten that far yet."

But there's something else that's important. Carter Frederick was afraid of the Badger.

Which means he's dangerous, if he scared a hard case like Frederick.

Rachel felt a spurt of dismay. *The Badger guy must know we were children from the project. If he can't find us through this guy, he'll use someone else.*

And then what? Kill us to get rid of the evidence of the doctor's experiments? Or maybe he thinks he can use us.

She shuddered. *Are you saying we have to give up the lives we've made for ourselves in New Orleans?*

For now. Until we can... His voice trailed off and he shrugged. *I don't know what the answer is.*

They had been focused so completely on the conversation that they hadn't noticed anyone on the road—until a man and woman came striding toward the parking area in front of the cabin.

Rachel gasped as she recognized them.

It was Mickey and Tanya. Obviously they had escaped from the warehouse—and had kept looking for her and Jake. Maybe they'd zeroed in on their psychic energy, now that they recognized it. And their session with Frederick had drawn them.

The newcomers didn't give them any warning, they simply attacked, sending a bolt of energy toward Rachel and Jake that would have knocked them over if they had been on their feet.

Rachel cried out. Jake grabbed her hand, grounding her.

He dived into the bushes, taking her along.

When she started to speak inside her head, he whispered, "Don't communicate that way unless we have to."

She did as he asked, wondering if it would do any good.

A bolt of power landed near where they'd entered the underbrush, then another close by. Both of them singed the leaves where they hit, but the foliage was apparently too damp to catch fire.

In the face of the assault, Jake froze, and she did the same.

Another bolt landed, but this one was farther away, and she knew that their attackers didn't know exactly where she and Jake had gone.

"I think it's because they can't zero in on us when they

can't see us and we don't use our powers," Jake whispered.
"And that includes speaking mind to mind."

That was good news—until they had to fight.

They crept deeper into the underbrush along the bayou,
tramping through standing water. It was strange not being
able to reach for Jake's mind, but she kept herself from doing
it.

When a snake slithered in front of them, they both went
stock-still.

Jake squeezed her hand as the reptile undulated out of their
way, obviously as alarmed to see them as they were to see it.

Stopping about fifty yards from the picnic table where
they'd been sitting, Jake cautiously eased up so that he could
look through a break in the screen of bushes.

He kept his voice low. "They're just standing in the parking lot like they don't know what to do. Mickey took a couple
of steps toward the bayou, and Tanya held him back. I think
they don't like the idea of getting up close and personal with
nature."

"Can we make it to the car and get out of here?" she asked.

"Maybe. But then what—fight them again the next time
they find us? They attacked as soon as they saw us. They
didn't try to negotiate or reason with us. We have to assume
that their goal is to kill us."

She nodded, hating to acknowledge that he was right. They
had to stop these people from coming after them, and this
was as good a place as any.

When she started to stand, Jake tried to restrain her, but
she gently took his hand off her arm. "I want to get a look at
them."

He made a low sound but didn't prevent her from easing
up behind a tree trunk and peering at the couple who were
arguing in the parking area.

They weren't speaking out loud, but she knew from their

body language that they weren't in agreement about what to do next.

When she hunkered down beside Jake again, she murmured, "Tanya's the leader. I think we need to focus on her."

Jake nodded. "Agreed."

"We practiced pooling our energy when we weren't touching. How far apart do you think we can get?"

His jaw tightened. "No more than twenty feet."

"Okay, I'll come out of the bushes and pretend I'm trying to reason with Tanya woman to woman. Then we'll hit her." She stopped and thought for a moment. "We should have a signal. When I say 'give up,' that will be the sign to attack her."

"Yeah, except that we're going to make a little change. I'll do it."

"No," she answered at once. "They'll see me as less of a threat."

He was silent for a moment, and she knew even without reading his mind that he hated her putting herself in danger again.

When he finally nodded, she went on. "And we keep our focus on her, no matter what they do. I mean, even if the attack seems to come from Mickey."

She turned and pulled Jake to her, holding tight for a few emotion-charged moments. Then she eased away, stood up and strode out of the bushes.

The other couple saw her almost immediately, and she put her hands in the air as if they were holding a gun on her.

"Don't hurt me," she called out. "I want to talk to Tanya."

The other woman jutted out her jaw. "Why?"

"Can't we speak woman to woman?"

"Where's your boyfriend?"

"He's hurt."

Tanya shrugged. "What a shame."

"Why are you doing this to us?"

Tanya kept her gaze steady. "Because as long as you're alive, you're a threat."

"If you kill us, it won't solve your problem. We came to Houma because Dr. Douglas Solomon had a clinic here where he was doing experiments—we assume on fertilized human eggs."

"Why?" Tanya demanded.

"He was trying to create children with superintelligence. That's where we came from."

"He was trying to make telepaths?"

"No. Like I said, he was trying to create superintelligent children. When his experiment didn't work, his backer shut down the project."

"How do you know all that?" Tanya retorted.

"We've been doing research. But the point is, he was getting his subjects by running a fertility clinic, and there were hundreds of children involved. Are you going to kill all of them?"

"Hundreds?" Mickey gasped.

"Be quiet," Tanya ordered.

"You can't kill them all."

"You're wrong."

Mickey had a sick look on his face, and Rachel figured he hadn't signed up for mass murder.

"Just let us go. We'll leave the country, if that's what it takes to satisfy you."

Tanya's eyes narrowed, and Rachel knew that an attack was coming.

She might have shouted aloud, but she thought there wasn't time. Instead, she called to Jake inside her head. *Give up.*

At the same time she dodged to the side and back, closing some of the gap between them.

She could feel the power gathering between them, but it was already too late for the attack she'd planned.

A bolt of energy slammed into her chest. Another whizzed past her as she fell back, feeling as if the air had been knocked out of her lungs. At the same time, her head spun and her vision blurred.

Behind her, she knew Jake wanted to leap from the bushes and rush to her.

Somehow she managed to shout, *No!*

If they got him, too, they were lost.

No, they were already lost. Mickey and Tanya must have been practicing their skills for a long time. They were stronger than she and Jake under the best of circumstances, and now she was lying on the ground with her head spinning.

Sadness and horror came down on her like a thick, dark cloud. Everything she had hoped for with Jake was lost. They should have run and figured out what to do next. They'd been crazy to stay here and fight.

She turned back toward Jake, but he was hidden from her.

Get away, she whispered in her mind. At least she'd have the satisfaction of knowing they hadn't killed him, too.

What happened next totally confused her.

Chapter Sixteen

Rachel heard a loud rustling in the bushes. A flock of large white birds took flight and flapped away. Then Tanya screamed.

Turning her head, Rachel saw an enormous alligator come creeping out of the vegetation along the bayou. Then another. Then the snake they'd seen earlier slithered into view, followed by a family of raccoons.

The raccoons ran past, but the other animals were slower and kept heading for the center of the parking area where the couple stood. As Rachel watched, she knew that Jake was doing it, sending a low level of warning energy through the underbrush, telling the animals to escape—and not toward the water.

While the predators advanced, Tanya and Mickey instinctively backed up into the underbrush, before sending a bolt of energy at the lead alligator, making it shudder and go still.

But changing their focus gave Rachel and Jake the edge they'd needed.

Even with Jake hidden from view, she felt him gathering power, and she helped as best she could. As Tanya and Mickey sent a bolt at another alligator, Jake flung a ball of energy toward Tanya. It caught the edge of the blast she'd sent at the alligator and hurled it back toward her. The double whammy had her staggering. She fell in a clump of weeds, her eyes wide with shock that these two novices had knocked her off her feet.

Jake was ready with a second blast, and Rachel struggled to help.

She braced for an attack, perhaps from Mickey, but he had gone down on his knees beside Tanya, his total focus on his fallen lover.

As they'd agreed, Jake ignored him, sending another charge at the woman who had directed the attack on them, and Rachel heard her make a gurgling sound.

Rachel lay on the ground, panting, sure that she could summon no more energy, but when she felt Jake reaching for power again, she gathered every ounce of concentration she could scrape together, adding as much as she could to the effect.

Ruthlessly, Jake launched one more bolt at Tanya, who shuddered, then went still.

Mickey leaned over her, cradling her in his arms, his expression urgent and terrified. He must have been trying to communicate with her, but he wasn't getting any answer.

He laid her gently on the ground, then raised his head and screamed, turning toward Rachel with a murderous expression on his face. She could feel him gathering energy on his own—without Tanya—and she knew he was going to strike her. She was too weak to fight back. Too weak to run. If he hit her, she was dead.

Before he could attack, Jake came flying out of the bushes. Like her, he must have used up all his psychic energy bolts, but he could still use conventional force.

Hearing Jake coming at him, Mickey whirled, but he was already on the ground, and Jake landed on him.

"See how you like this."

Grabbing Mickey's head, he smashed it against the ground. The other man tried to fight back, but he was no match for

Jake's rage and physical strength. Mickey had been relying on psychic abilities for so long that he'd lost any physical-fighting skills he might have once possessed.

In the face of the onslaught, he went limp, and Jake rolled off him, then ran to Rachel, gathering her to him.

"Are you all right?" he asked, his voice filled with urgency.

"I think so."

She was still weak and confused, but she felt no more threat from the couple who had followed them here, intending to kill them.

Jake held her for long moments, then eased away and ran to Tanya, who was lying in the weeds, pale and still.

"Is she dead?"

"Yes," Jake replied. He turned just as Mickey pushed himself up. Rachel screamed, thinking he was going to attack Jake, but he ran in the other direction, into the underbrush, and disappeared. Was he trying to get away? Or kill himself now that Tanya was dead? Or was he too disoriented to know what he was doing? She heard him tramping through the foliage, followed by a splash, then thrashing in the water, the sounds of a man who couldn't swim.

She thought about going after him. He would drown if she left him there. Or an alligator could get him.

But Jake caught the thought and answered.

He and Tanya came to kill us. He'll try again if you go after him.

Yes, she managed to answer, hating herself.

Stop! We're finally free of them. Think about that.

She knew he was right. Struggling against her normal compassionate impulses, she pushed herself up and swayed on unsteady legs, looking around.

When another figure appeared on the road, she stiffened. It was the man from the office.

"You folks okay?" he asked.

"Yes. Why do you ask?" Jake said aloud. In his mind he was saying, *Nothing happened here. Nothing happened here. Go back to what you were doing.*

Rachel added her power to Jake's. For a moment the man hesitated, then he turned and walked back the way he'd come.

When they were alone again, Jake turned her toward him, and she leaned against him.

"It's over," he murmured. "They can't hurt us now."

She allowed herself to absorb that for a few moments. "But Carter Frederick is still on the bed."

He cursed. "Yeah, we still have to take care of him. Somehow."

"I'll bet his fingerprints are in the room where he killed Evelyn."

"It was a hotel room. There were probably lots of prints."

"But his should be included."

"So we drive him back to New Orleans and turn him over to the cops?"

"Let's give him the good news."

"What about the other guy? The Badger."

"I don't know."

When they stepped into the room, Rachel's eyes went to the man on the bed. The covers were rumpled, as though Frederick had made a violent attempt to get away. But he'd failed, and he was still cuffed and tied to the bedposts. Now he was lying pale and still, and she remembered the energy charge that had whizzed past her when she'd dodged aside. It must have zinged through the door and hit Frederick.

"Oh, no," Rachel whispered.

Jake rushed to the kidnapper and pressed a hand to his neck. "He's alive."

"We've got to save him. I want to turn him in to the police," she heard herself say, disgusted with the idea of helping him even as the words came out of her mouth. "I want him to tell the police he killed her."

"Why would he do that?"

"Because it will be his best alternative."

She moved to the other side of the bed, putting her hand on the man's shoulder, struggling to overcome her revulsion at touching him. He'd tried to kidnap her. He'd tried to choke her, and it was so tempting to simply let him die. But she couldn't do it.

Jake's eyes went to her. When he started to speak, she shook her head.

I don't want to take a chance on his hearing anything we say.

Right, Jake agreed. *He's in bad shape. Can you save him?*

I don't know.

You've connected with your clients on a deep level. Maybe that was why you could bring me back when I was dead.

That was different. I love you.

Their eyes met across the man on the bed.

We might hate this guy, but we need him alive. For us, Jake said. *What should we do?*

Pour energy into him.

Even saying that made Rachel recoil, but she reached for Jake's hand. When his soul had left his body, she'd gone after him and brought him back.

Do you have the strength to do it after the way Tanya zapped you? Jake asked.

I don't know.

I'll help.

She grimaced. When she'd known Jake was dying, she had pressed herself to him to get as close as possible. She could barely stand to touch Carter Frederick.

The idea of reaching out to this man sent a shiver of fear through her, but she pressed on.

Closing her eyes, she sensed energy building between herself and Jake. It was a comfort to feel him there. He was with her, every step of the way.

Still, she knew she had to do more than pump energy into Frederick if she was going to accomplish her goal.

When she clenched her jaw, she felt Jake soothing her.

It's okay. Do your best.

No, I'm going to do this, she answered, knowing that his giving her permission to fail made a difference.

She swallowed hard, then reached for Frederick's mind.

As she caught the edge of his consciousness, she gasped. Dark memories enveloped her. Some of them were violent. Others were sad. By herself, she would have jerked back for self-protection, but Jake kept her grounded.

She saw Carter Frederick as a boy, saw his father pounding him with fists, then saw the boy stamp down the sidewalk and kick a dog that was tied to a tree outside a house.

She rejoiced with him when he made friends with another kid in the neighborhood, then felt his despair when the family moved away. Her heart clutched when his mother died, leaving him alone with a father who turned more and more to the bottle, then took out his anger and frustration on his son.

She saw him in school feeling stupid when he couldn't understand a lesson, then shrinking back as a teacher yelled at him in front of the class. He got his revenge by slashing the teacher's tires.

More scenes followed. A girl he thought he loved who broke up with him to date a more popular boy.

There were scrapes with the law. The young man robbing a convenience store.

Drugs. Another girlfriend. He ached to connect with her, but he couldn't keep his violent impulses under control. He hit her. She left him. He was going to track her down, but her brother was large and threatening, and Carter thought better of tangling with the guy.

He never finished high school. He hooked up with other young toughs. Took jobs for crime bosses—then found his way to legitimate businessmen who wanted jobs done that they couldn't acknowledge.

When he'd gotten a call from someone whose alias was the Badger, he'd been pretty sure the guy was dangerous. But he paid well, and Frederick always completed the assignments he was given. And he made good money for his efforts. Enough to live in a nice apartment.

Until he was sent to get information from Evelyn Morgan. She'd tried to fight him off. Tried to get away, and she'd ended up dead. But that hadn't been Frederick's intention.

He'd failed, and he'd been afraid of the Badger. He'd never met the man, but he knew it would be fatal to disappoint him, which was why he'd been so relentless in his pursuit of Rachel and Jake.

And she knew he hadn't been lying to her. He had never met this employer. He had dealt with the man only over the phone, but even at long distances the Badger tied Carter's stomach in knots.

His fear of the Badger came through very clearly. Along with the memories flashing through the man's mind.

And overlaying everything was a more engulfing fear. He was dying. But he wasn't going upward toward the light. He was sinking into darkness so profound that it rose to swallow him up.

You don't have to go there, Rachel whispered to him.

He startled. *Who are you?*

Rachel Gregory.

He tried to wrench himself away from her.

No. Let me stay. I'm here to help you.

How?

You can change everything. Give yourself another chance.

Impossible.

You can make a fresh start. Your life doesn't have to go on the way it has.

She had started this because she wanted to help herself and Jake. As she understood Carter better, she wanted to save him—with a desperation she would have thought impossible. Because she had left Mickey in the bayou? Perhaps.

Carter was speaking again.

I'm dead. I'm going to the bad place.

Not if you want to change.

Maybe he believed her. Maybe he was so terrified that he would grasp at any straw. But she felt a shift within him. He'd had so few good relationships. So few good impulses. Now she was reaching out to him in a way that pulled him toward what he might have been if his life had been different.

She'd started off hating and fearing him, but the connection changed her perception.

In the background, she heard Jake speaking urgently to her.

Don't trust him. He'll hurt you.

She couldn't answer Jake, not and focus on Carter.

Open to me, she begged the unconscious man. *Let me show you what it can be like.*

She wasn't sure what she was doing. She only knew she was showing him possibilities he had never even considered. Each bad thing could have come out differently. Each decision could have been the turning point.

As she tried to show him that, she felt him pulling back from the abyss.

The dark forces clawing at him loosened their hold, and his spirit came back to the body lying on the bed.

Her own body jerked as life swooshed back into him. Blinking, she looked down at him. He was sleeping.

Tell him what will make a difference for him, Jake whispered in her mind.

Go to the police, she said to Carter. *Tell them that you were trying to question Evelyn Morgan. Tell them that she died trying to get away from you. It was an accident. You didn't mean to do it.*

He moaned.

I know you don't want to go to the police, she soothed. *I understand. But you don't want to go to the dark place when you die. You want to change your life. Take your punishment. Then find a job where you work for humanity.*

She didn't know if it was possible. Maybe he'd already gone too far down the wrong path.

You think he'll go to the cops? Jake asked.

Maybe. If we reinforce him.

Carter still slept, and she was exhausted from connecting with him. Jake came over to her side of the bed and caught her in his arms, carrying her to the chair by the window, sitting with her cradled in his lap. She closed her eyes and leaned her head against his shoulder.

"Tell him to stay asleep," Jake murmured.

She did as he asked, sending Carter soothing, restful thoughts and the suggestion that he didn't want to wake up yet.

"We have to get him back to town," she said to Jake.

"We've got other problems first. Like, there's a dead woman lying in the weeds."

She dragged in a strangled breath. "Would you believe I wasn't thinking about that?"

"You were a little busy."

"What are we going to do?"

"What they would have done to us. She's already dead. I think we can leave her for the alligators."

Rachel fought a wave of sickness, but she didn't have a better suggestion. He was right. Mickey and Tanya would have killed her and Jake and let the creatures of the swamp cover up the crime.

Still, she didn't offer to help when he strode outside. Through the window, she watched him pick up Tanya and carry her into the underbrush where they'd taken refuge when the other couple had attacked.

When he disappeared from view, she waited tensely until he returned—alone.

"I put her in the water with Mickey," Jake said when he reappeared.

"Did you see him?"

"No. But I saw a couple of gators."

She winced. "What about their car? They must have left it somewhere."

He shrugged. "Maybe they went hiking and got into trouble."

"Maybe."

"If it's on the side of the road, nobody may check for several days." He looked out the window. "But Carter Frederick's car is still outside."

She nodded.

"I'll drive it back to the city with him in it."

"Is that safe?"

"We'll tie him up again and lay him on the backseat, just to be safe. You drive the car we came in. And we'll meet up…" He paused to think.

"In the parking lot between the French Market and the river."

"Kind of a conspicuous place."

"But not too far from a police station."

Rachel walked back to the bed and bent over Carter Frederick.

We're going back to town now, she told him. *Everything's going to be all right. You're going to turn yourself in to the police. You're going to tell them that you were hired to get information from Evelyn Morgan, and she got killed when she was fighting with you. You didn't mean to kill her. It was an accident. You'll feel so much better when you explain it to them.*

He moved restlessly on the bed, and she reinforced the suggestions she'd given him.

"Let's go," Jake said aloud.

"I'd better put my wig back on," Rachel answered.

"Yeah. Right."

He waited while she made herself look like the woman who had driven here with him. When she was ready, he stepped to the bed and helped Frederick up. She steadied him on the other side, and together they walked to the kidnapper's car.

After they'd laid him on the backseat and secured his hands and feet, Rachel told him to sleep on the ride back to the city.

When she was finished, Jake closed the back door and opened the front.

Rachel came into his arms, and they held each other tightly for long moments.

"I don't like separating," she whispered.

"I don't like it, either, but we've got to drive both cars back to town."

"Unfortunately."

Jake backed out of the space in front of the cabin. She did the same, then followed him down the access road to the highway. When she lost sight of him around a bend, she sent him a mental message.

Everything okay?

She felt his startled reaction. *You can still reach me?*

Yes.

That's good. We won't be out of touch on the road.

She followed him onto the highway, keeping him in sight. It took too much effort to stay with him the whole way, but she checked in with him from time to time, until they'd both pulled into parking spaces beside one of the pavilions of the French Market where vendors sold produce, hot sauce, Mardi Gras masks, T-shirts and other New Orleans souvenirs.

Since it was late in the day, the lot was almost empty. Jake wiped his fingerprints off the steering wheel and the interior of the front seat while she opened the back door and uncuffed Carter Frederick's hands.

Jake leaned into the other side of the car and worked on the man's feet.

When he was untied, they helped him sit up. Then they both wiped away any remaining fingerprints and walked into the market, where they stood behind a nearby pillar and looked out toward the car.

It's time to wake up, Rachel said gently.

From her hiding place she saw Frederick blink and look around.

Who's talking?

Rachel Gregory. You were going to get information from me, but you changed your mind because of what happened to Evelyn Morgan.

Alarm contorted his features. "She's dead."

But it was an accident. You want to tell that to the police. You want to come clean because you don't want to end up in the bad place when you die. Do you remember that you were on your way there when I pulled you back? It will be for all eternity next time.

He shuddered, and she knew he was remembering the

horror of what had happened when she'd snatched him back from the brink of death.

Jake grasped her hand, giving her a silent message, and she glanced at him before looking back at Carter Frederick.

You're going to forget that I talked to you. You're going to forget that you found us in Houma. You never left New Orleans. You fought with us here. You tried to kidnap me here. But you never caught up with us again.

"Will that work?" she whispered to Jake.

"I don't know. But we have to try."

She sent the same messages to him again, then ended with words of encouragement. *You're very brave to turn yourself in. But it's the best thing. You want to change your life because you don't want it to end the way it almost did. You should go right to the police station now. It's on Royal Street. You'll feel so much better when you tell them about the accident with Evelyn Morgan.* Rachel waited a beat before asking, *Do you know how to get to the police station at 334 Royal Street?*

Frederick nodded. Then, as they watched, he climbed out of the car and looked around as though he had just realized where he was. Or maybe he was looking for them.

Rachel heard Jake gasp.

"What?"

"He's got a gun. It must have been hidden somewhere in the car." He cursed.

"Can we get it away from him?"

"We can't take the chance."

Before Frederick got more than twenty yards from the car, a uniformed policeman stepped out of the French Market and into the parking lot.

Frederick saw him and froze.

Then he raised the gun.

Oh, no! When Rachel started to dart out from around the pillar, Jake held her back.

Stay here. You can't do anything.

She knew he was right. She'd only get them arrested.

Then the sound of gunfire made her gasp.

Chapter Seventeen

Jake fought against the sick feeling rising in his throat. They'd expended a lot of time and effort setting Frederick up to turn himself in. Apparently, his criminal instincts were too strong. As soon as he'd seen a cop on the street, he'd run.

Leaving Jake and Rachel where?

Jake heard the sirens. Was it police cars, or maybe an ambulance? Maybe the guy wasn't dead, after all.

Jake ached to step out from behind the pillar and find out what was going on. Instead, he linked his fingers with Rachel's, leading her in the other direction.

"Where are we going?" she gasped out.

"To an apartment over one of my antique shops."

"Is that safe?"

"For a while." *I hope,* he silently added.

They walked down the street at a normal pace, even though he wanted to get out of sight as soon as possible. As they turned down a side street, he felt safer. They wended their way toward the antique shop, then stopped short when he heard a radio blaring from an apartment.

"City police have shot an armed man in the French Quarter. According to authorities, the suspect drew a gun when he saw a patrol officer, and the officer opened fire. The injured man has been taken to Saint Luke's Hospital in critical condition."

Rachel gasped. "We have to go there."

"What are we going to do?"

"I don't know. But I feel like it's important."

Jake clenched his teeth. "We can't. We have to lie low until it's safe, then get out of the city."

"And then what?" Rachel asked.

"I don't know!"

Rachel gave him a pleading look. "Please, let me go to the hospital. It's important, but I can't do it by myself."

He grimaced. "We can't."

"I have to."

"One of your tarot-card-reader hunches?"

"Yes." She looked so serious that his throat constricted.

He didn't want to go anywhere near the hospital, but he felt Rachel's urgency coming off her in waves.

"Okay," he muttered.

She clenched her hand on his arm.

"Thank you. And don't tell me it's my funeral."

The hospital was in walking distance, and they approached cautiously.

Now what? Jake asked, still wishing that they'd gone to the vacant apartment.

You know everything about the city. How do we get in?

Walk in the front door, like we're there to visit a relative.

He felt her cringe.

Did you change your mind?

No. She took his arm, and they went through the oversize revolving door and into the main lobby.

Rachel moved along the wall, her gaze turned inward.

What are you doing?

I need to focus. Her urgency made him keep any further

observations to himself as he watched people come and go. At least nobody was paying them any attention.

He was still taking in the busy lobby, when she spoke again.

The woman at the front desk is occupied. Pick up the two visitor's passes that a man and woman just left on the counter.

Jake blinked, looking toward the desk as a man and woman walked away. While the clerk's back was turned, he picked up the passes and kept his body angled away from the desk as he returned to Rachel. She clipped on her badge, and he did the same as she led him toward the elevator.

They'd come here to find Carter Frederick. And Jake was thinking that if the man was alive, he was in the emergency room, or being operated on. So why were they going up to one of the wards?

But Rachel had a head start on psychic talents, and she must be operating on some knowledge that he didn't possess.

He sensed her excitement but couldn't catch her thoughts.

In the confines of the elevator, he tried unsuccessfully to read her expression, before he asked, *Rachel?*

Her thoughts gave away nothing. Cryptically she only told him, *Let's see if I'm right.*

He went along with her.

They got out on the third floor, and he followed her around a corner and down a hallway. When he saw uniformed police officers stationed outside a door, he wanted to run in the other direction, the way Carter Frederick had run, but he wasn't going to leave Rachel.

"We're expected," she said to the officer.

"Names?"

"Rachel Gregory and Jake Harper."

Jake stiffened as she gave their names. What was she

doing, leading them to the cops? But the officer only nodded and stepped aside.

Confused yet intrigued, Jake followed Rachel into the hospital room and stopped short when he saw a woman lying in the bed. Her head was wrapped in bandages, but when he stared at her face, he felt the shock of recognition. It was Evelyn Morgan.

In the chair beside her was Detective Paul Moynihan.

"You're alive." Jake gaped at the woman who had come to his office.

She looked as if she had aged ten years since he'd seen her last.

"And very lucky. I was in a coma," she said in a halting voice. "They didn't think I would wake up, but I fooled them."

"I see you got my message," Moynihan said to Jake.

"Which message?"

"The one I left this morning on your voice mail and with your assistant—where I told you it was safe to come out of hiding."

Jake nodded. He hadn't gone near his voice mail or contacted his assistant today, but he preferred not to explain how they'd arrived at the hospital.

Instead, he gave Moynihan a dark look. "Why did you say Evelyn Morgan was dead?"

"We decided that if someone wanted her dead, we'd let them think they'd succeeded."

"We were wanted for murder," Jake accused.

"Questioning."

Jake hardened his stare.

"And we still didn't know you weren't involved—until Evelyn woke up and told us about the guy who came to her hotel room and demanded information about an international terrorist plot she'd never heard of."

"International terrorist plot?" Rachel breathed. She kept her gaze on Evelyn, but her mind zinged to Jake. *It wasn't that, was it?*

Apparently she doesn't want to tell the real story.

"Why were we at the top of the suspects list?" Rachel asked the detective.

"Because you both had appointments with her for just before she was attacked."

"Call me a sentimental old matchmaker," Evelyn broke in. "But I met Rachel Gregory when she did a tarot card reading for me. Then I was at Jake Harper's restaurant and met him, and I thought they'd be perfect for each other. I was horrified when I found out I'd gotten the two of you in trouble."

Jake stared at her, and their eyes met. She was lying, but the expression on her face told him that she wanted him to keep the confidence.

Don't complicate the story, Rachel silently added, and he knew that starting to explain the real facts would only get them into deep trouble.

"I do so apologize," Evelyn said.

"No harm done," Rachel answered quickly. "While Jake and I were on the run from the police, we got to know each other pretty well. I guess your instincts about us were right."

"Since you were innocent, why did you run?" Moynihan asked Jake.

"Because I've seen too many people railroaded into jail," he answered. "It's easier to prove your innocence if you're free."

Evelyn ignored the exchange as she looked from Rachel to Jake and back again, then smiled. "You found out what you have in common?"

"Yes," Rachel answered.

"I'm so glad."

She looks like butter wouldn't melt in her mouth, Jake silently observed.

But she's a tough-as-nails old broad.

Jake turned to Moynihan again. "If there are no charges against us, then I think we'll be going."

"Wait. I want to talk to you," the woman on the bed called out.

"You probably should rest now," Jake answered, knowing he was going to stay as far away from her as he could. When he turned and left, Rachel followed him out of the room.

You don't want to ask her some questions? Like why did she start the fire at the clinic? Rachel asked when they were on their way back to the elevator.

I want to get as far away from her as I can.

Maybe she knows the Badger's real name. It's likely she was working for him out of D.C. when she torched the building.

Or she was working for Solomon. Maybe he wanted to get rid of his own clinic. If he's still alive, he could be dangerous. And suppose she does know the guy who funded the clinic. What if he's the one who sent Carter Frederick after her? What's he going to do when he finds out she's not dead? If I were her, I'd go into hiding. Like us.

Rachel sighed. *That's probably smart.*

When they reached the lobby it was quite a different scene from when they arrived. Several camera crews and reporters had set up shop there. Ducking to the side, Rachel and Jake waited until a young brunette reporter began to give her stand-up.

"A man who drew a gun on a police officer earlier today and was shot by the officer has died. He was not carrying identification, and his identity is still unknown. He is believed to be in his early thirties. A white male with blond hair and blue eyes. The name of the officer involved in the shooting is being withheld, pending an investigation."

"Carter Frederick's dead," Rachel breathed.

"Unless this is another police scam."

"Why would they...?"

She shrugged, then made a small sound. Not wanting anyone to hear their conversation, she continued silently. *I guess he went to the bad place.*

Probably where he belongs.

He was scared of what was going to happen to him.

You don't feel sorry for him, do you?

I can't help it. He was so frightened.

Not frightened enough not to try and shoot a cop the first chance he got.

They left their visitor's badges on the counter and stepped into the twilight.

Where are we going? Rachel asked.

To the apartment I mentioned.

They were each lost in their own thoughts as they walked back to the heart of the French Quarter. The entrance to the apartment was around back, and as they reached the stairway leading upward, Rachel realized that she hadn't heard much of what Jake was thinking.

You're learning to block me, she said.

I think you did it at the hospital before we got to Evelyn's room.

I was trying.

It's a good skill to have in the long run.

They walked up the back stairs to the apartment. The key was on the top of the door frame, and when they stepped inside, Rachel saw the place was beautifully furnished with antiques that must have come from the shop below.

She breathed out a little sigh as Jake closed the door behind them.

"I'd like to say we're safe," Jake said. "But what I said before still counts. We've got to stay in hiding until the situation with the clinic is resolved."

"It will be. Maybe not this week," Rachel murmured.

"How do you know?"

"The same intuition that made me think that Evelyn Morgan was alive and in that hospital room."

"Nice to be able to sense the future."

"Actually it's strange to have a sense of my own future. I never did before."

"You mean you didn't know we were destined for each other?"

"I would have been a lot happier if I had."

Yeah. He pulled her into his arms, holding her tight. *I love you. I want to marry you, have a life with you.*

Oh, Jake!

He lowered his mouth to hers for a passionate kiss.

"How long will we have to stay in hiding?" he asked when they finally came up for air.

"Get me a deck of tarot cards, and maybe I can tell you," she answered, gathering him close, still amazed that she and this fantastic man were together.

Would they have been, without Evelyn Morgan?

She was beginning to think so. She and Jake would have found each other, and she was sure others from the project would do the same.

What would happen when they connected as she and Jake had? Would they turn out like Tanya and Mickey, or would they be friends? She longed to know, but that information was beyond her.

We'd better be cautious if we meet any more of them, Jake advised.

Yes.

She turned her mind back to Jake, the man she loved. The

man she had thought she would never find. But here they were, in each other's arms. With the rest of their lives stretching before them.

* * * * *

In the darkness, he couldn't see her face, but he didn't need the sense of sight to know what she looked like.

He lowered his head, and as his mouth touched hers, he was caught by a blaze of need that radiated to every cell of his body.

They'd gone from strangers to intimates in seconds. Without understanding why it had happened, he wanted her. Right here. Right now. Out in the open.

Those heated thoughts and the pain pounding through his brain almost wiped out his ability to think, but not quite. Somewhere in his consciousness, he understood that what they were doing was dangerous. That knowledge was as sharp and insistent as the desire binding them together.